Annie knew the time had come to tell Jared about her past.

"Adoption saves so many children from never knowing love," she said, and began gathering the courage that had allowed her to contemplate marrying him. "You're adopted. You know how well it can work. You'll be able to help the three children through any transitions they have to make."

She opened her mouth to tell him the secret only two other people had known, but the dark expression on his face, and the narrowing of his blue eyes, stopped her.

"My life turned out better than I could have hoped when I came to live with the Campbells," he said, an odd note of emotion gone before she could identify it.

"But I will never understand how a mother— any mother—can give up her child."

MARY KATE HOLDER

is a transplanted Aussie now living in sunny Florida. She married her husband four years ago after meeting him online in a karaoke chat room. They live with their dog and three cats who laze around the sunroom all day and think the Florida climate is so much better than rural Australia's temperatures. When she's not writing, Mary Kate likes to putter around in her garden or go fishing and is slowly learning to do home improvements—but it's not quite as easy as it looks. She also is now a full-fledged karaoke fiend.

SECOND CHANCE MOM

MARY KATE HOLDER

Steeple
Hill®

Published by Steeple Hill Books™

STEEPLE HILL BOOKS

Steeple
Hill®

ISBN 0-373-87315-8

SECOND CHANCE MOM

Copyright © 2005 by Mary Adams

This edition published by arrangement with Steeple Hill Books.

® and TM are trademarks of Steeple Hill Books, used under license. Trademarks indicated with ® are registered in the United States Patent and Trademark Office, the Canadian Trade Marks Office and in other countries.

www.SteepleHill.com

Printed in U.S.A.

He gives the childless woman a family,
making her a happy mother.
—*Psalms* 113:9

Chapter One

Annie Dawson sat alone in the crowded restaurant. Today could very well change her whole life and bring her back into her little boy's life. Toby…a child she'd thought she had given up forever.

What was he doing today? She looked out one of the large windows at the glorious sunlight, and blue sky in the distance. Was he outside right now playing with his brother and sister?

There wasn't anything more pretty, more filled with possibility, than the lazy days of an Australian spring.

"Annie?"

Startled from her thoughts, she looked up at the sound of her name. Deep blue eyes, narrowed and questioning, surveyed her.

"It's been a long time." She shook the hand he held out to her. He pulled out a chair and sat down.

Jared Campbell hadn't changed a lot over the years.

His face still wore that serious look. Even as a boy he had seemed far too somber.

The dark suit was perfectly tailored. The shirt seemed even whiter against the bronze of his skin and the dark green tie was a conservative splash of color. From the top of his dark head to the tips of his shined shoes—about six foot four if she didn't miss her guess—he exuded the confidence of a man in total control of his world.

Clean-shaven, yet there was just a hint of five-o'clock shadow on his lightly tanned face. His hair, a deep brown with gold flecks scattered through it, was cut short on his neck.

She felt helplessly casual in her knee-length khaki skirt and plain white cotton blouse that buttoned down the front.

"I apologize for being late. There was an accident on the motorway and traffic was stopped for miles."

He filled her water glass and then his own from the crystal carafe on the table. He picked up his menu. "Would you like to order now?"

Annie nodded, ravenous despite the apprehension that twisted and tightened her stomach. In a few minutes their waiter arrived, scribbling down their order before hurrying off.

"I'll admit right now I'm a little nervous," she said.

"There isn't anything to be nervous about," he replied calmly. "Just tell me about yourself."

She bit her bottom lip, wondering how it was that he didn't already know everything there was to know about her.

"You've lived in Guthrie all your life, Jared. I know how well the local grapevine works. You probably know all there is to know."

Being reminded of the life she had tried so hard to leave behind made her sad and angry. The sadness was a natural emotion. The anger was something altogether different. She struggled with it many times, calling on the Lord to help her let it go.

"Do you have any contact with your mother?"

"I haven't seen her in almost a year."

He frowned. "She doesn't visit you?"

"My mother spent years trying to forget I existed. Why would she be interested in me now that she isn't legally required to be?"

"She still drinks?"

"She did the last time I saw her," she said truthfully. "It has ruled her life for as long as I can remember." Alcohol was the only friend and companion she could ever recall her mother wanting.

"I'd like to know why you agreed to do this. I'm not offering money and I know for certain what I'm getting out of the deal. But Lewis wouldn't reveal anything about your reasons for agreeing to marry me."

Annie smiled at the mention of their mutual friend, the lawyer who knew more about her than anyone alive.

"You know what my childhood was like. Just about everybody in the town knew. Do you remember all those times you'd come home from football practice and I'd be at your house?"

He nodded. "You were so quiet, you barely said two words."

"When your sister joined the Big Sisters' mentor program at school, she changed my life. I could look in her eyes and not see the pity I saw from others."

"Sara always had a big heart."

"She made me feel like I mattered. She was the sister I never had. Now I have a chance to do something for her."

He seemed to contemplate her answer for a few moments. "I know from what Lewis told me that you attend church. Faith has always been important in my life. I attend church regularly. Sara and James made sure it was a part of the children's lives, too."

Annie liked the easy way he spoke about his faith. It was refreshing. Lately, professing it had become very out of fashion for a lot of people.

"Sometimes faith is all you have and then you realize it's the one thing that is always there…that and hope."

He nodded. "So…you feel at peace with your decision to marry someone you're not in love with?"

Annie had thought long and hard about that very thing. She had prayed to find the peace and resolve she now carried in her heart about it.

"Marriage is a partnership, as the ceremony says, not to be entered into lightly…not to be falsified."

"There are some people who would agree that was what we were planning to do…if they knew."

Annie clasped her hands together on her lap. "I believe our reasons for getting married are valid. We are trying to keep three children together in the only family environment they have ever known."

Annie wanted to do this…she was meant to do this and not just because it would give her back the one person it had torn her heart out to be parted from.

"If we get married for the sake of the children, Jared, we're not mocking the sanctity of marriage. We aren't in love with each other, but we share a commitment to family and I'm sure we can be friends."

"Why do you feel so strongly about the kids?"

"Because of the childhood I had. I'm in a position to help them have a life that I wished for every day, and I want a family to care for," she said honestly.

"You sound very certain."

"I am."

He looked at her as if seeing her in a new light. "You're very young. Just twenty-one?"

"Yes."

"I'm thirty-three," he said. "I remember what it's like to be your age. What a person wants at twenty-one won't automatically be her goal when she's twenty-five. I need to be sure that you won't suddenly get the urge to travel or take off for some other reason and leave the kids. They need stability."

Annie needed that, too—a place to belong, somewhere to be needed. She had wanted to go back to Guthrie for so long, to replace bad memories with good ones. Now faith had shown her the path she felt sure she was meant to take.

"I was an adult by the time I was twelve, Jared. There's

nothing like watching your mother sober up after a three-day drinking binge to make you grow up real fast."

When he didn't reply she ploughed ahead. "I'm not afraid of hard work. I can do any domestic chore you can think of. I can cook, I can keep a nice house and I love children."

Annie leaned forward. "I won't let you down. I won't run off and leave you because there isn't anywhere I want to go. My goals may change, Jared, but if you choose to go through with this, my commitment, to those children won't. And if you want me to sign a legal and binding agreement, I will."

Annie sat back in her chair. The ball was squarely in his court. She had messed up once in her life, had lost her faith, but God had given her a chance to make amends. And when she told Jared the main reason she wanted to marry him, Jared would see why it was so important to her.

When their meal arrived, Annie ate with reserved delight. It seemed Jared appreciated his meal with the hearty appetite of a man used to hard work and home-cooked food. And he must work hard. His long, lean body—all flat planes and masculine angles—showed not an ounce of fat. He was toned and healthy.

"No legal contracts," he said finally, watching her eat for a few seconds more before giving her an indulgent half smile that threatened to take her breath away.

She paused, fork in midair. "I'm sorry, is something wrong?"

"It's refreshing to eat a meal with a woman and not

have to watch her nibble on lettuce leaves and celery sticks like a martyr." Approval showed in his expression. "You like your food."

"Absolutely," she said, smiling for the first time since he'd arrived. "It comes from being nine years old and never quite sure when the next meal might be. I learned to appreciate it when I had it."

He surveyed her silently for what seemed like an eternity. "You really did have a horrible time of it growing up, didn't you, Annie?"

She heard no pity in his voice and that was just as well because she didn't need any. She wasn't that helpless child any longer. She made her own decisions, lived her own life.

She had come a long way from that horrid little shack with its dingy walls and stained, fading carpets. "No worse than a lot of other kids—and I survived."

He thought about her answer for a moment then asked, "Is there anything you wanted to ask me?"

"Why did you tell the social worker you were planning to be married?"

He looked up from his meal and Annie almost fell off the chair when one side of his generous mouth lifted in a genuine smile.

"Desperation. Caroline and Luke are foster children. Sara and James were in the process of adopting them both."

"Are they blood siblings?"

"No. Caroline's mother gave her up to the state when she was five," he said, his look hardening. "The man she married didn't want any other children in his house except his own. He gave the woman a choice…him or Caroline."

Annie was stunned. "How could she choose a man over her own child?"

"I gave up asking why a long time ago. All I know is that little girl has brought a truckload of joy and sunshine into our family. It's that woman's loss and our gain."

There was a fierce determination in his tone. He wasn't giving any of these kids up without a fight.

"Luke's mother was unmarried and apparently very sick for most of the time she had him. When she died he became a state ward, too."

"Lewis said to see them together you would think they had been brother and sister their whole lives."

"That was the kind of love Sara and James instilled in them. The same as our parents instilled in Sara and me when we were adopted."

That two children born to different families and raised by two loving, gentle people could become as close as Jared and his sister gave her hope that Toby, Caroline and Luke could find that, too.

"Toby's adoption went through soon after he was born. Sara and James named me as legal guardian in their will."

If he noticed her sudden stillness, the way her breath caught and held, he made no mention of it.

"I don't want to be married, Annie. But if that's what it takes to allow me to adopt Caroline and Luke myself, then that is what I'm prepared to do."

"I know about your aversion to marriage. Lewis told

me you would rather have your teeth pulled without anesthetic than say the words 'I do.'"

Jared smiled slightly. "He knows me well."

"But what happens if you meet someone and fall in love, if you meet 'the one'? It won't be very convenient being married to me."

"I believe in love, I believe in what my parents have, in what my sister and her husband had," he said resolutely. "But I also believe it isn't for everyone. My commitment to the children is the most important thing in my life."

That commitment was evident. "How is your dad?"

"The cancer is in remission and the doctors are optimistic."

"I'm pleased," she said sincerely.

"Any other questions?"

"Not a question, really…"

"Go on."

"Lewis said you do have a sense of humor, but I'd need a pick, a shovel and funding from a major mining corporation before I found it."

His lips twitched but he managed not to give in to a smile, which, judging by the two he had already bestowed on her, was a real shame.

"Lewis is a good friend and a fine lawyer but he talks too much." He motioned for the waiter. "Are you ready to leave?"

Annie nodded. She reached for the bill but Jared beat her to it, casting a frown that would have intimidated a lot of people in this room.

"Call me old fashioned, but when I take a lady out for a meal, *I* pay the bill." He left enough to cover the cost and a generous tip. "If we go ahead with this, you'll find I'm old-fashioned in a lot of ways."

Annie felt a surge of pleasure to know that the man who very well could be her future husband believed in chivalry.

"You mean like opening doors, and waiting until a woman is seated before sitting down?"

"Among other things," he replied, tucking his wallet back in his trouser pocket. "So if you're a rabid feminist who believes men shouldn't protect their women or try to make life easier for them, now is the time to say so."

"I can live with that. Just so long as you remember that I'm no wilting violet, Jared. I'm capable, intelligent and more than willing to pull my own weight."

"I think we'll make a good team," he said finally. "Lewis told me you don't have a vehicle. I'll save you the bus ride and drive you."

The drive back to her apartment in the city was slowed down by rush hour traffic. "How big is your farm?" she asked.

He checked the rearview mirror of his four-wheel-drive truck and indicated before changing lanes. "Dad's place has thirty thousand acres but I'm also working the land that James and Sara owned and it's about the same size. A lot of it is just grazing land and some of that I lease out to other farmers, but I've got crops in."

His words sparked a memory and Annie smiled.

"When I was young and Mum was passed out I'd climb the big hill behind our old house and sit there looking out at the fields. The purple Patterson's Curse. Yellow rapeseed. The brown of newly turned earth. And then the green fields. It always reminded me of a patchwork quilt."

"You and my mother will get along like a house on fire. She calls our little corner of the world God's canvas. According to her, the shades of nature are His watercolors and the goodness of men is His inspiration."

"Your mother always was a wise woman. Very few people take the time to see the world like that."

"She's one in a million, all right."

Later, when she was alone, she would sort through her emotions, but she couldn't help but wonder what his life had been like before the Campbells had taken him into their family.

"What kind of animals do you have?"

"Sheep, milking cows, hens and horses."

"Milking cows?" she queried. "You milk them and use it?"

That got an amused grin out of him. "Where did you think we'd get our milk?"

"I was hoping you'd say you stock up regularly from the store in town. I guess it's too much to hope that you don't butcher your own meat."

He chuckled again. "Afraid so."

He pulled into the parking garage under her building.

"Once we're married—if we get married—will you teach me about being a farmer's wife?"

"You won't need teaching," he replied, his eyes softer, his voice a deep baritone. "You'll learn it as you live it."

He got out of the vehicle and came around to her side, helping her down and escorting her to the elevator. As they waited, Annie knew the time had come to tell him about her past.

"Adoption saves so many children from never knowing love," she said and began gathering the courage that had allowed her to contemplate marrying him. "You're adopted. You know how well it can work. You'll be able to help them through any transitions they have to make."

She opened her mouth to tell him the secret only two other people had known, but the dark expression on his face, and the narrowing of those blue eyes, stopped her.

His jaw was clenched tight. "My life turned out better than I could ever have hoped when I came to live with the Campbells," he said, an odd note of emotion gone before she could identify it.

"But I will never understand how a mother—*any* mother—can give up her child."

A chill of foreboding washed over her. He was deadly serious. She could barely breathe. How could she marry him and keep the secret? She couldn't lie, not to him, not about this.

A marriage built on a lie was set down on a foundation that would in the end crumble and hurt many people. Lies festered and boiled inside a person like an open wound.

Yet the alternative was to tell him and see the look

of disgust on his face. He would call the whole thing off. She would not get to be a mother to the children. She would not be able to repay Sara for the friendship and the love she had shown her. *Please God,* she prayed silently, *don't let this fall apart now.*

Her heartbeat accelerated. Her hands began to tremble ever so slightly and she realized why Lewis had suggested she not tell Jared about her past.

"You make adoption sound like the easy way out."

"Isn't it?"

The elevator pinged and opened for them. She pushed the button for her floor and waited, watching him, her breath lodged somewhere in her throat, her palms sweating.

"I look at Sara's children and I know I'd die for them. I'm not even related by blood. How can a mother who gives birth to a child not have those same feelings…even stronger ones?"

The words were out of her mouth before she even thought about it. "There are cases, like Caroline's for example, that are horrifying, but there are women out there who do it out of love for their children."

She continued on, not even realizing how it might sound to him; she just said what was in her heart. "Giving up a child you love, never to see him or her again, is one of the most difficult decisions a woman in that position has to make."

His gaze locked with hers instantly and Annie knew this was the moment to make her choice…to tell him and end it now or to keep silent about her past, about

Toby, and try to live with the guilt she knew would compound day by day.

"I've watched television programs on adoption, read books written by woman who have gone through it…I even know a woman who did it," she said quietly, swallowing the half truth and hating the aftertaste.

His expression remained as dark as it had been since the discussion was started. "But still they hand their children away like consolation prizes in a raffle."

"I think you would find most mothers try to find a loving family who can give the child everything she isn't in a position to."

"Or doesn't want to be bothered with."

Annie wondered if his jaw would actually break, it was clenched so tight. Then he looked down at her, his blue eyes a darker shade than before, his mouth set in a grim line.

"We aren't ever going to see this from the same side of the fence, Annie, so you had better know that now… before we go any further."

If she told him about her past he would turn and walk away. If she stayed silent about her past, Annie would have to reconcile it within herself and deal with the consequences the lie would bring…and they would come.

With a prayer in her heart, she made her decision, already feeling the first tentacles of guilt wrap around her. "Then I guess we had better make it one of those topics we agree to disagree about."

"You won't ever change my mind on the subject."

His tone told her it would be a waste of time trying. "Tomorrow is Friday. I'd like to pick you up and take you back to Guthrie for the weekend. I'd bring you home Sunday. You need to meet the kids, spend time with them. I can't really make a decision before I see you with them in their environment."

Annie swallowed all her reservations and concentrated on why she was doing this. For Sara and James. For three children who were a family.

"Friday sounds fine."

He ushered her out of the elevator as they came to her floor. "I almost forgot." He extracted three wallet-size photographs from his pocket. "These were taken at Sara's birthday party a week before she…died."

"Thank you. It was thoughtful."

He nodded. "I'll see you tomorrow afternoon about four? We can be home for the dinner my mother will no doubt cook."

"I'll be ready and waiting."

"Be sure to pack a pair of sturdy boots and maybe a pair of jeans, too. The kids like nothing better than playing outside. I'll be seeing you."

Annie went inside her apartment and shut the door. Kicking off her shoes and tossing her purse onto the sideboard, she looked down at the photograph that was on top.

Caroline was beautiful even at age nine. Hair so blonde and eyes so blue she would one day have some man wrapped around her little finger. Luke's dark hair was curly and his big brown eyes were filled with life.

His smile shone through…infectious and wide. He was seven.

Annie hesitated as she came to the last photograph in the pile, turned facedown. She put it right side up.

She had counted every day of the last eighteen months. In the silence of her apartment, her heart hammering like a runaway freight train, she sat and stared into the beautiful face of the little boy who was her son.

The son she'd given to her best friend to raise.

Chapter Two

"Has she changed very much?"

Jared loved his mother dearly, but just the fact that he was entertaining the thought of getting married—and to Annie—had her smiling every time she saw him these days.

"She's older."

Eve placed her hands on her hips. "Very funny."

"Don't go getting mushy."

"My son shows the first sign of interest in a woman in more years than I care to count and he expects me not to be happy about it?"

Jared sipped the coffee she'd poured for him, the homemade chicken pot pie settling warmly in his stomach.

"I was honest with Annie," he told her. "She knows what kind of marriage this will be if we decide to go along with it."

Eve came back to the table to sit opposite him. She

reached over and touched his hand. "I want you to be happy. Life is…so short."

Since the tragedy they had all leaned on each other a little more, drawn their strength from their faith, from God and the love and closeness of family.

He'd never seen his father cry until the day they'd buried Sara and James. They had all known the first year was going to be the most difficult. They'd had no idea it would mean fighting the system to keep their family together.

He marvelled at how his mother never looked any older. Her curly light brown hair was cut in a style that flattered her. Her blue eyes were as kind and gentle as he'd always known them to be. Her smile could warm any heart.

"Keeping Sara's family together will make me happy."

"You took a lot on yourself when your father got sick. You gave up your life in the city to come home and run the farm. We appreciated that. And now what you're doing for the children is wonderful…."

"But…?"

"You go through life with such a single-minded determination, caring for everyone else." She shook her head. "I thought things would work out with Melanie."

Jared hadn't thought of his ex-fiancée in a long time. The sad thing was that her leaving had barely caused a ripple in his life.

At the time, he'd accused her of wanting too much

out of their relationship. Now he realized any woman he became involved with would be like Melanie.

They would want the parts of him that he dared not share, parts that he had locked away a long time ago. They would want him to make himself vulnerable and to trust them. He hadn't trusted his heart and soul to anyone in so many years. He didn't believe he ever would again.

He wanted what his parents had, but was unwilling to pay the price…opening himself up completely to the love of another person.

His mother sighed into the silence. "We hoped when you got married it would be for love…like your father and me. Like Sara and James."

"I'll be fine, Mum. I promise. Besides, there are reasons other than love to get married. Good, sound reasons."

She didn't reply but her expression told him she thought it was a load of hogwash. "Just be kind to this young woman, Jared. She has a very loving heart to want to do this for the children. Annie was always very sweet."

"You'll be happy to hear that she hasn't changed in that respect." He finished his coffee. "I'm going to take the kids home."

"It's so quiet in there. I can almost guarantee your father is asleep."

When they entered the living room, Jared smiled at the scene. Caroline was sprawled on her stomach in front of the television. In the armchair, Mick Campbell cradled both his grandsons, one on either side. Luke's eyes were closing slightly as he fought sleep. Toby had given up all pretense and was snoring softly.

His father had always been a tower of strength—active and energetic. Then as he'd fought cancer Jared had watched him fade to a shadow of the man he'd been…at least on the outside. On the inside, the fight of his life had made him so much stronger.

Eve went over and began waking the boys, her husband stirring instantly.

"Sorry I fell asleep."

"You need your rest," Jared said. "Besides, it kept the boys quiet."

Caroline turned around and she smiled at her uncle. "Can we get a scarecrow?"

"How about we get a lion and a tin man, too?"

She sat up, brushing long strands of hair over her shoulder. "That would be silly," she told him, her expression one of infinite patience. "We have nowhere to keep a lion and what good would a tin man be on the farm?"

"I'll think about the scarecrow."

His mother cleared her throat. "You do realize she thinks that is as good as a definite yes."

"I know. But the day will come when she's asking for a car. I figure I'll indulge her while I can afford it."

Caroline was already starting to get the boys' things together. It took ten minutes to get slippers on feet, robes on over pyjamas and backpacks in the car.

As Jared buckled Toby in his car seat, Caroline

helped Luke with his belt. He turned to his mother and father, both standing on the veranda.

Mick had his arm draped possessively around his wife and Jared saw what he did every time he looked at them together—a love that had taught him a lot growing up, a love he'd wanted to find someday. A love that he knew was always going to be out of his reach because he wasn't willing to take the risk.

"I'm bringing Annie to dinner tomorrow night. She'll stay the weekend."

Eve smiled. "She can stay with us. I'll make up the spare bed and give her the extra key so she can let herself in if we go to bed early."

"Thanks, Mum. I figure being here even for a few days will give her time to get comfortable with the kids…and them with her."

His mother cast a glance at Caroline in the front of the vehicle. "You need to think about what you'll tell them, too. You can't just introduce another woman into their lives and not expect resistance. Toby and Luke will probably be okay with Annie but…Caroline may need time."

Jared scratched his head. "That's going to be the tricky part."

"Not to worry, son, you'll find the words when the time comes."

Jared nodded. "I hope so, Dad."

As they drove away, the boys eventually fell back to sleep. Caroline searched for her favorite music station on the radio.

Jared's thoughts turned to Annie. He remembered a

lot about the life she had lived as a child. Her father, a hardworking farmer by all accounts, had died one month before her birth. Some people blamed Annie's neglect on the fact that her mother had been so traumatized by the loss of her husband that she couldn't bring herself to love her daughter.

It wasn't for him to judge the woman...that was God's right. But he felt heartsick every time he thought of the quiet, sad little girl Annie had been.

Back then there wasn't a year that went by when child welfare didn't arrive on the doorstep because of reports. Three and a half years ago, Annie had left town and nobody had heard anything of her since. He wondered if she even knew that her mother had packed and left soon after she did, or that the house of her childhood had burned to the ground?

Annie had been a surprise today, not at all what he'd expected. Her innocence had shone through but so had the little things he couldn't help noticing. She was an attractive woman. The green of her eyes reminded him of an ancient jade statue he'd seen once at a museum while on a school field trip.

He'd expected her to be taller. For a woman who stood only five feet four she seemed far too fragile for life on the land. Even her hands had been impossibly petite, her fingers touched up with clear nail gloss. There was a gentle way about her.

His mother could play matchmaker all she wanted. He would never be any good as a husband, at least in the traditional sense.

Maybe his father was right. Perhaps he did let his past dictate his future more than it had a right to. But how did a person leave it behind? How did a person turn and walk away from beliefs so ingrained that even a loving family couldn't banish them?

There wasn't a day that went by that Jared didn't wonder why his mother had started to hate him and blame him for everything that went wrong in her life.

Today he had been as honest with Annie as possible. All the way home to Guthrie he had allowed himself to imagine the life they could have…one built around the children.

Jared knew this weekend would be the test.

Once they arrived home, he put the boys into bed, knocking on Caroline's door as he passed by.

"You can come in, Uncle Jared."

She sat in the middle of her bed brushing her hair. She had the sweetest face and a gentle smile. Somewhere there was a woman who would never see this girl grow into a young lady, achieve, succeed and be happy. Jared would never understand. He had given up trying.

Caroline had been close to him before her parents' death, but now she was his shadow. He'd even noticed that she'd tried to assume more responsibility. On more than one occasion he'd had to sit her down and remind her that he was the adult. She could still be a big sister, he had told her, but she didn't have to try and be a grown-up, too.

That would come far too soon.

He'd wanted her to understand that she didn't have to carry any burden, that her childhood was precious.

"I have something to tell you." He sat down on the edge of her bed.

She looked at him, moisture in those big blue eyes, her chin quivering just a little. "Is that lady going to make us go away?"

Jared reached out and touched her hair, wanting to give her comfort, wanting her to feel secure. "No, she isn't. But that is part of the reason I went into the city today."

She waited, wide-eyed, a cautious expression on her face, her hands stilled now and resting in her lap.

"I'm bringing someone home this weekend to meet you and the boys. Her name is Annie."

"Is she going to be our baby-sitter?"

"No, but I'm hoping she'll be my wife."

Caroline looked toward her window, eyes fixed on the night sky outside. "I didn't know you had a girl-friend."

Jared called on all his patience and love to help her understand this. He was the only person she would trust to explain it to her.

"I don't. I knew Annie when she was a little girl. She was a friend of your mother's." He reached out to cup her chin in his hand, bringing her gaze back to him.

"Caroline, she's a good person and she wants to help me take care of you, Luke and Toby. I promised you I wouldn't let you all be split up and sent away. I'm doing everything I can to keep that promise."

"Then let her be our baby-sitter or our nanny. You don't have to get married!"

"Sweetheart, nothing will change if I get married."

She cast him a dark look. "Everything will change," she said, placing the hairbrush on the nightstand and pulling her knees up to her chest.

"Caroline, this won't be like when Janice got married," he said, knowing she didn't call the woman her mother. That word was reserved for Sara alone.

She looked back at him. "I want to be by myself now."

He'd handled that like a real pro! Caroline had pulled up the drawbridge and set her walls in place. Jared just had to pray he hadn't lost her trust or confidence.

He leaned over and kissed her forehead, then reached out to turn off the bedside lamp.

"Leave it on...please." Her voice was so tiny, her tone unsure and tinged with a fear he knew only time and love would banish.

"You look like Rudolph."

Annie looked across the desk at Lewis Devereaux. He'd grown up in Guthrie. He was a family friend and had gone through both high school and university with Jared. He was funny, compassionate and he told it like it was. He was also the one person Sara had trusted to handle Toby's adoption. Since then he'd been a good friend to Annie.

"It's been an emotional twenty-four hours."

"Was I wrong to tell him you wanted to see photos?"

Annie shook her head. Lewis was such a sweet man. He might try to pull off the hard-nosed lawyer attitude but it never worked with her. He was a big-hearted softie but he had sworn her to secrecy when she'd mentioned it to him.

"It's probably a good thing that I get this out of my system now. I can just imagine what kind of look I'd get from Jared if I burst into tears the minute I saw Toby."

"The lunch meeting must have gone well. He's told me to get all the paperwork in order so, barring any unforeseen events this weekend, you two can be married as soon as possible."

He gave her a look of admiration. "I have to say, I didn't think he'd go for it once you told him about Toby."

"I didn't get to tell him. And I found out why you told me not to."

Lewis looked thoughtful. "And I can see you're already beating yourself up about not telling him."

"Lying is wrong. Not only that, but it just makes more problems."

"You could look at it from the other point of view."

Annie raised an eyebrow. "Which is?"

"It wasn't a lie…it was an omission."

She shook her head and wiped her eyes and nose again. "It's a lie no matter what way I look at it, Lewis, but there isn't anything else I can do. It's for me to reconcile within myself…if I can."

"Jared is a good man but a little too closed off when he wants to be. Nobody gets close to him easily. And he has a lot of baggage, most of it to do with his birth mother."

"That's what I don't understand. The Campbells gave him a good life. He told me that himself. He saw how the lives of those children improved when Sara and James adopted them. How could he be so shortsighted about it when it brought good things into his life?"

Lewis came around the desk, propping his hip on the edge of it. "He's seeing it from the other side. You know what it's like to have to give up a child. He was a child given up. And he wasn't a baby. He was almost a teenager."

Annie blew her nose again. She felt sad for the child he had been and for how it had affected the man he was today.

"It's like I told you at the start, those children need you. Jared needs you, too. It doesn't matter why he's marrying you. The fact that he's willing to do it to keep those kids together is a start."

She left his office determined not to cry as she walked to the bus stop at the end of the block. People rushed by her, but Annie didn't notice them.

The tears would come at different times. She hadn't been prepared for these emotions. It was a searing heat in the region of her heart…the feeling of a pit opening up, ready to swallow her whole.

She would never have entrusted her child to anyone else but Sara. Annie had known for many years of Sara's plan to adopt children when she married.

When the time came to make the decision on her

baby's future, she had made the right one. Annie had also asked Sara not to tell her family that she was Toby's natural mother.

There was always the chance she would for some reason return to Guthrie. She hadn't wanted them to be uncomfortable or worried that she had come to take him back. She'd moved to the city long before conceiving Toby and nobody in Guthrie had known of her condition except Sara.

That was how she wanted it to stay.

Not telling anyone had just seemed better and Sara had respected her wishes. Now Annie was glad she had made the decision to keep it a secret between them. Jared would never have understood why she'd given her child away.

Her child. She savored those words, wondering why life had turned out this way. Fate had given her the chance to be his mother again.

How ironic that all she had ever wanted was within her reach because of a freak car accident that had killed Sara and James Monroe just six months ago.

Annie reached into her bag. She stared at the photograph again. Her doubts banished the guilt for now, as she gazed into eyes the same color as her own and wondered what it would be like to hold Toby in her arms for the first time.

Jared couldn't help but smile when Annie opened the door to him that Friday afternoon. She wore a pale green lightweight cotton short-sleeved shirt, faded blue jeans and sturdy thick-soled boots. Her hair was pulled back into a loose ponytail, wild tendrils escaping to frame her face.

"You can take the girl out of the country," he said, approval in his tone. "But there's always a little country that you can't take out of the girl."

Annie let out the breath she'd been holding. "I want to make a good impression."

"You don't have to impress anyone."

"I'm meeting your parents after a long time, and the children for the first time."

Jared smiled. "My parents will love you."

She picked up on what he did not say. "And the children?"

"Let's talk about it in the car." He reached for the small suitcase she had at her feet. Only when they were pulling out of the parking garage did he speak.

"I told the boys at breakfast this morning. Toby is too young to understand. Luke asked if you were pretty and if you could cook."

She smiled. "And Caroline?"

"She's going to need some time. Caroline's afraid that when we get married it's going to be a repeat of her past all over again, that something will happen and she'll be pushed out, not wanted."

Annie felt for the little girl. How horrific that memory must be for her. "We'll just have to prove to her every day that it won't be the same."

"It's not going to be easy."

"I know, but if I can show them all I'm not a threat,

that I'm not going to take you away from them, it will give us something to build on."

"Until I spoke to Caroline I never realized that they might feel threatened by someone new."

Annie turned slightly to face him. "Right now you're the focal point of their lives. Of course they are going to be protective of your time and your attention."

"Like you said, we'll just have to make sure they know they come first."

Annie cast a covert glance at him. He had dressed casually today. Moleskin trousers in a dark brown color, work boots with a thin film of dust on them and a crisp white shirt, unbuttoned at the neck. He was a very handsome man, his looks striking. He looked like an advertiser's dream for country living.

For the next hour, conversation touched on many topics—politics, world affairs, different jobs they'd had. But both stayed away from personal questions, as if by silent understanding that the other person would not welcome it. Finally, she stifled a yawn.

"I'm sorry, Jared, I've not been sleeping a lot lately."

"We've still got a ways to go. Why don't you recline the seat and get some sleep?"

Annie did, but each time she closed her eyes her mind wandered back to a different time, back to the day she'd turned her back on Guthrie and walked away.

Seventeen and lost, angry with her mother and with God, Annie had traveled a path of loneliness, living mostly in shelters. Whenever she did find work, she made just enough money to get a room. They were barren and stark, usually with just a bed and a washbasin.

Then Chris had started working at the fast-food restaurant. He was kind and he smiled a lot. He became a special person in her life. They found in each other somewhere to belong if only for a while. He was estranged from his family for reasons he never did want to talk about.

The day she'd found out she was pregnant, excitement had warred inside her with fear. Angry as she had been at God, Annie had tried to live a life of His teaching. Still, in her heart she knew something as joyous as a baby couldn't be a bad thing. It was God's creation, just as she was.

She never did get the chance to tell Chris he was going to be a father, never would know what he might have said or done. Death had taken him from her life as quickly as he had come into it. Something as simple as a coughing fit turned too quickly into a fatal asthma attack. By the time she'd gotten to the hospital, he was gone.

The days after his death were still a blur to Annie. She had found it hard to cope with the grief. Each day it threatened to suck her into a black hole.

She was unskilled, with no high school diploma and no prospects of ever getting one. Suddenly having a baby on the way and being alone had caused her to make some tough decisions.

Toby might not have been a planned baby, but to the seventeen-year-old girl who had carried him inside her, he had been her guiding light. Because of Toby she had found her faith again. She began to trust the Lord again, realizing that when she had run from Him, He had not abandoned her, but had waited to welcome her back into His love.

Toby had made her want to be less selfish than her mother, to want more for a child that deserved something other than a life of poverty and struggle in a dingy, hole-in-the-wall bedsit.

There had been times during her pregnancy when she'd convinced herself she could raise a child alone. But the memories of her own childhood, of going without things she saw other children take for granted, were still so fresh in her mind and her heart.

She had wished away her childhood because it had been so bleak, without color and sound and laughter. Growing up had meant getting out, looking after herself. Having a life.

Envy was a sin, she knew, but oh, how she had envied the children, even the ones who had made fun of her with her charity clothes and shoes a size too big for her.

As the time to give birth to her child had drawn nearer, the nightmares had started—images of her child's life being as miserable as hers had been. What kind of life could they have in the shoebox she lived in? What would she use to buy food and clothes and toys if she couldn't work?

Sure there were handouts but she had lived like that with her mother. She remembered nights without dinner and days when her mother had drank until she slept for hours.

In the end, Annie admitted to herself what she'd been denying for nine months. She wasn't about to take a chance with her baby's future.

The cycle would stop with her, she had vowed. Her child would have something better. Jared thought it was easy for a mother to give up her child, but he didn't know the nights she had spent crying herself to sleep.

It had taken a long time but Annie had finally stopped beating herself up about the decision she had made. At the time it had been the right one for her child.

Her mother had never taken Annie to church but she had found it on her own, and Sara had taken her many times. When she had been at her lowest and most desperate for guidance, for direction, she had found peace and a safe place to rest her weary heart.

Her faith had sustained her through the pregnancy and through the ordeal of giving up her son. Now that same faith filled her, and Annie felt it in her heart that God was giving her a second chance.

This time she had to get it right.

"Annie, wake up. We're here."

Jared almost hated waking her. She'd looked peaceful though a few times she had mumbled words he hadn't been able to understand.

She came awake adjusting her seat. "Jared, it's beautiful."

He saw it every day of his life and still the beauty of this place and the scenery took his breath away, made him thank God.

They got out of the car and stood in the dusty driveway. The homestead wasn't a mansion, just a place to call home. It was a solid structure of white weatherboard and dark green trim. The veranda ran the entirety of the house. The house was nestled in a grove of native Australian trees, some of them still quite young, some a little more firmly rooted in the soil.

He wondered how Annie saw it. Would she be taken by the beautiful wattle tree with its prominent yellow blooms, the eucalyptus with their strong scent?

"Most people see the isolation before they see the beauty."

"They must be blind."

"Come on inside."

"The children?"

"At my parents' house."

Part of her was grateful for the reprieve and part of her was anxious to see Toby.

As they walked to the house, Annie caught a movement out the corner of her eye. The dog was obviously old, and it didn't move very well.

"That's Murphy."

She crouched down as the dog, not at all wary of her, approached. "What breed is he?"

"Good question…and one we've been asking since we found him curled in the shearing shed as a puppy. He looks like he's got Australian kelpie in him."

His deep black coat shone with health and his eyes were pale gray. He nuzzled the hand she held out and then moved a little closer to her and allowed her to pet him.

"How long have you had him?"

Jared crouched down beside her and Murphy instantly went to him, their body language speaking of a long, close friendship.

"Sara and I found him about thirteen years ago. She kept him when I went away to the city. He became the family pet when they got the kids."

They walked toward the house, Murphy following them. "Any other animals I should try to win over?" she asked cheerfully.

They climbed the steps and Jared held the screen door open with his foot while he unlocked the front door. "We have numerous guinea pigs and rabbits out the back. We also claim one very irritable old cat and two young mousers we keep in the shed."

Annie nodded. "The house is lovely."

In the living room the furniture looked well-used but lovingly cared for, the floors a shiny wood. The kitchen was a sunny room with yellow-and-white spotted curtains and the same motif on everything—from the potholders to the water glass sitting on the sink.

"Sara liked sunflowers."

Jared moved behind her. "Yeah."

"They are such happy flowers, don't you think?"

Jared shrugged. "I've never thought of a flower being happy but I guess they are."

"You have a huge vegetable garden out there. And so many other flowers."

If there was such a thing as heaven on earth, Annie was sure she'd found it. Back in the entryway, Annie noticed the family tree chronicled on the wall as she made her way slowly up the stairs.

It was a progression of photographs and portraits, some with an old sepia tone, some more modern black-and-whites and eventually color.

She took the stairs slowly, one at a time, meeting one generation after another. There were pictures of Sara in her youth—her smiling face and bright eyes, the blond hair and cheerful tilt to her head as she looked at the camera.

James, very tall, a little quieter looking and a serious teen. Pictures of them together, from high school graduation to weddings made a part of Annie both happy and sad.

Happy that they had found each other, sad because they had built the foundations of a good life and would not see any of the seeds they had planted grow to fruition.

"The family portraits are cute." Jared came up behind her. "I often find myself looking at these here."

Annie moved down the steps. Her heart clenched and her throat became tight as she looked at the portrait of them all together dated just one year ago.

Sara and James sat in the middle, Caroline beside her mother, hugging close. Anyone who didn't know would take them for biological mother and daughter. Luke sat by his father, holding his hand and looking just a little shy. On Sara's knee sat Toby, looking straight at the camera with eyes Annie would have known anywhere.

Her son was happy in this photograph, content. He was smiling and his life stretched before him was secure and full of promise.

"The world was lucky to have had your sister and her husband, if only for a little while."

Jared remained silent and Annie understood. She made no more comments. She turned, leaving him to gaze at the photographs, caught up in his own memories.

Chapter Three

He discovered her in the laundry room moments later. "We have a clothes dryer and a line outside. I don't know which you prefer."

Annie smiled. "I hated doing my laundry in the city. Those dryers do their job but that crisp, new scent of outside is missing."

Jared nodded though he didn't reply. To him, dry clothes were dry clothes. As long as they were clean and accessible he was happy.

"This is where the kids play." He led the way outside. "The trampoline is Caroline's favorite."

Annie had asked Santa for a trampoline for many Christmases growing up. Then at age nine, her mother had given up all pretense of there even being a bearded gift giver. After that little bombshell, Annie had stopped wishing.

There was a large swing set that combined aspects of a jungle gym, as well. "You put sand around the bottom of the play set."

"James did. I swear they were the most safety-conscious parents of all time." Annie heard the pride in his statement.

"The chicken coop is past the vegetable garden. We let them roam free every day and they get housed at night."

Annie smiled. "Free range eggs."

"They're the best." He walked a few more steps. "That row of coops over there houses what my mother calls 'the critters.'"

"Should I ask?"

"Remember the rabbits and guinea pigs I mentioned before?" She nodded. "James put a lot of work into their living quarters."

"I'll bet the boys love their guinea pigs."

"Actually the boys have the rabbits. The guinea pigs belong to Caroline. Now she's bugging me for a ferret."

Annie stopped. "Aren't they dangerous?"

"They are if they get near the rabbits."

"Is she getting one?"

"I might be able to divert her. She wants a scarecrow now…and she mentioned ducks a few weeks ago." He walked a little farther. "The flower beds need to be replanted in places and the seasonal vegetables are going to be ready in a month of so."

In twenty minutes, Annie's life had changed. This was where she was meant to be. It didn't matter what reasons had brought her here, what events had transpired to bring her into Jared's life.

"I could make a home here," she said honestly, taking in a deep breath of clean country air.

Jared turned and looked at her, a satisfied expression on his face. "I'm glad you think so."

Annie wasn't about to rush over any bridges only to have them burn behind her. "We'll see how things go in the next few days."

Jared nodded. "Come on. We don't want to be late for dinner."

The ride to his parents' farm took her past stretches of road and landmarks she remembered.

"You look nervous."

She nodded reluctantly. "I am a little…okay, a lot."

"You know my parents already."

"Do they know you're thinking of marrying me…to keep the children together?"

"Yes."

Annie felt even more nervous now. His parents were good, kind people who in recent years had been through their share of struggles. But for them to know their son was marrying and not for love…

"Annie, they will support me in any decision I make if it's what I want." He slowed the vehicle and smiled. "Besides, it's too late to back out now. We're here."

The Campbell farm was as she remembered. The house was small and neatly kept, the gardens just as tidy, though now they were full of what would probably be the last blooms of the season.

This is where the circle of love had started. The Campbells, unable to have children of their own, had adopted Sara and Jared. And so had begun the events that had brought Annie here today. She took a deep breath as they pulled to a stop and got out as the front door of the house opened.

"You're just in time for dinner."

Eve Campbell looked a little older but was still a petite, casually dressed farmer's wife. Annie felt a little of her anxiety ease as the smiling woman came toward her and enveloped her in a hug the likes of which Annie hadn't felt in a long time.

"Welcome home." She looked at Annie just like a mother hen checking her chick. "We've missed you."

Annie had been waiting to say something to this woman for a long time. "I've never forgotten how kind you were to me, the dinners I had here and the gifts you bought me," she said, squeezing the woman's hand. "I want to say thank you."

Eve blinked back moisture in her eyes. "Your smile told me that a million times over." She took a good look at Annie. "You've grown into a very beautiful young woman."

Annie blushed, not even trying to stop the heat that surged into her cheeks. She touched the end of her ponytail where it lay over one shoulder.

"I never did get the blonde hair I longed for as a girl, or the brown eyes…and the freckles didn't go away."

"Child, your beauty is natural. Your skin is so smooth and flawless and those green eyes…just striking."

"I'll try to remember that."

"And freckles?" She scoffed as if it were a minor concern. "It's features like that which make people truly interesting…make them stand out from the crowd."

Jared came around the truck and hugged his mother. "What's for dinner?"

"A lamb roast, with vegetables and homemade damper."

He laughed. "I should bring company home more often."

"I haven't had a home-cooked lamb roast since I left Guthrie. And I've forgotten how damper tastes."

"Your taste buds are about to get a refresher course. Mum makes the best bread."

Eve led the way into the house and before Annie even walked into the homey, aroma-filled kitchen she could hear the laughter of children—a boy and a girl—and the voice of an older man.

Suddenly her palms were sweating and her heart felt as if it were lodged somewhere in her throat. It was pounding so loud she was afraid it would just stop beating.

On legs that were threatening to go numb, as the realization of what lay ahead tonight hit her, Annie followed Eve into the kitchen, Jared behind her.

"Toby got hungry and after I fed him he just went out like a light," said Eve. "He'll be awake soon, I expect."

Another reprieve—or torture—Annie couldn't decide which.

Was she really ready to see her child? No, not her child—maybe biologically, but she had to remember that if she remained in these children's lives that was the way it had to be.

At the table sat Mick Campbell. To his left sat Caroline and Luke, and there were three empty chairs waiting to be filled.

Jared could feel the tension radiating from Annie. "Dad, you remember Annie Dawson from Rivers End Road?"

Mick stood up.

"Nice to meet you again, sir."

He chuckled, though it ended in a cough that had Annie wondering just how long it was taking him to get over his illness.

"Nobody's called me sir since…I can't remember when. Call me Mick."

"Okay."

Jared turned his attention to Caroline, who sat with her head down and eyes glued to the plate in front of her.

He began with the easiest task.

"Luke, say hello to Annie."

The little boy used the back of his hand to wipe a milk mustache from his top lip and grinned, showing that his two front teeth were missing.

"Hi."

"It's nice to meet you, Luke."

"Are you our new mummy?"

The question exploded into the silence of the room.

Nobody spoke. Annie could feel their unease at the implications of that innocent question.

It was Caroline who broke the silence. "Mummy died. We aren't getting another mummy." She raised her eyes to look at Annie. "We don't need a mother."

It was as much of a warning as Annie would have needed had she been the kind to try and come into their lives and take Sara's place.

"Caroline—"

Annie put a hand on Jared's arm and he fell silent. "Well, how about a friend?" She slid into a chair opposite the girl who glared at her with a militant expression. "Could you use a friend?"

Her expression didn't change. "I have friends."

Eve made a quiet sound of distress. Mick sighed heavily and Jared took the situation in hand. "Annie is going to be here for the weekend."

"You're going to marry her, you said so," Caroline accused. Eve moved about the kitchen busying herself serving dinner and Mick shot Annie a smile of support.

"We won't be getting married unless Annie likes it here."

One little eyebrow raised and Annie knew the gauntlet had been unwittingly thrown down. Something told her Caroline would do her best to make sure Annie didn't like it here. What Caroline didn't know was that Annie had been a scared, lonely little girl once.

"This looks wonderful," Annie said as Eve put the roast in the middle of the table and Mick handed the carving knife to his son.

After a brief prayer, Jared carved it with expert movements and precision before taking a seat alongside her. The roast was complemented by fresh damper, hot out of the oven, and a casserole dish filled with what Annie knew were farm-fresh vegetables.

Eve put the juice on the table and filled Annie's glass. "Dig in, everyone. We don't want it to get cold."

The meal was enjoyable except for Caroline's stony silence. If she were asked a question she would nod for yes or shake her head for no. If the question required an actual answer, she would shrug.

Luke however had no such qualms. "Do you like to play?"

Annie smiled at the boy whose blue eyes held mischief more playful than problematic. "I sure do."

"What games do you like?"

"Are we talking inside or outside games?"

"Outside."

"Um...horseshoes, cricket and building sand castles."

Luke's eyes went wide. "We have a sandpit and I can teach you to build really great castles."

"I'd like that."

He smiled so wide Annie wondered if he would hurt his face. But he had such wonderfully expressive features. He was a beautiful child.

Mick cleared his throat. "So Annie, Jared tells us you've been working in the city since you left Guthrie."

"Yes, s—" She caught herself just in time and smiled. "Yes, Mick. I'm a waitress at one of the more popular restaurants down there."

Annie wasn't worried about admitting she didn't have a job requiring a degree or diploma. The Campbells weren't the type to look down on others for any reason.

"Tough job, waitressing. Mother did it for a while after we were first married," he said, looking at his wife.

"I didn't like it," Eve admitted with a soft smile. "But we were newlyweds and back then we worked together for what we wanted."

As it should be, Jared thought, watching the tender byplay between his parents, longing unfurling in him for something he knew he would never have, something he desperately wanted to experience. If he was honest with himself, and Jared always tried to be, he could let himself have feelings for the woman he was thinking of taking as a wife.

She was everything a man could want in a wife. Sweet and gentle, intelligent and caring. And there was a kindness about her that was as genuine as she was. Yes, she had a past but so did he, and Jared had no doubt that her past had molded her into the woman she was as much as his had molded him.

Jared ate dinner, glancing at Caroline now and again and listening as Annie and his parents kept the conversation going. Even Luke listened intently to what was being said and every now and then he would ask Annie a question. Caroline preferred to eat her dinner in silence.

He remembered how wary she had been of everyone when Sara and James had first brought her home. The changes had been achingly slow, but each one had been celebrated.

Patience and love had brought Caroline through the nightmares and out of the darkness into the sunshine where little girls belonged.

Jared recalled the first time she had hugged him voluntarily. Up until that day she had always tensed when someone—anyone—hugged her.

Luke had been so different. He had thrived in the attention from a loving family. He was an affectionate child at heart and would warm to anyone.

And Toby, well, Jared loved them all, but the baby had taught him a lot about what it took to be a parent, even a fill-in guardian.

Annie would work at developing a relationship with Caroline…it was just her nature. He could tell Luke had already befriended her the way they talked about adventures they had yet to have.

But he wanted to see her with Toby. He was so young and confused by the sudden loss of his parents. There was something about Annie that told him she would be a good mother.

He wondered how much of that shy little girl still lived within Annie. Did she remember the times when his mother had taken out homemade pies and casseroles to her house, trying to make sure she had something in her belly before bedtime?

Jared remembered. He remembered going out to that dingy old house with his mother, seeing the sad little girl sitting on the broken porch steps in grubby clothes and shoes that were falling apart. He remembered walking into this house and seeing her sitting with Sara, the two of them pouring over a book or some project. He remembered with a smile the day his mother had bought her a brand-new dress to wear to a mentor meeting with Sara.

The tears welling in her eyes didn't start to fall until she saw the brand-new shoes to go with it. It was a credit to her that she had survived and become the person sitting here with his family now.

Mick said something funny and they all laughed. Jared found he liked the sound of her laughter. In fact he hadn't yet found anything he didn't like about Annie.

These children were relying on him to do what was best for them all. He felt it very strongly that Annie would fit in here.

He had prayed over his decision to take a wife for reasons other than love. He had prayed and he had found a peace with his decision to go ahead with his plan. He knew of marriages that were based on nothing but passion or, worse still, monetary gain. How could a marriage based on friendship and family be wrong?

Jared knew in his heart that Sara would approve.

"You got quiet all of a sudden, son."

He was dragged back to the present in time to see that Annie and his mother had cleared the table. All except his plate.

"Just thinking, Dad."

Annie almost dropped the plate in her hands when a fussing noise came from the other room. Eve dried her hands and left the kitchen.

Annie took a deep breath and she heard the woman come back in. "You finally get to meet the youngest member of Sara's brood."

Time had never stood still for her. Not when her mother had screamed in anger and sent her to bed hungry. Not even when the welfare people had come and put her into temporary foster care until her mother dried out. But now time stopped.

She had counted every day since his birth. Standing there in the Campbell kitchen, her heart hammering like a runaway freight train, she stared into the beautiful face of the little boy who had changed her life.

Annie couldn't help the smile that touched her lips. The beating of her heart was no longer a thundering cadence.

His hair was a deep brown and he was dressed much like his brother and sister, in blue jeans and a T-shirt. He wore socks but not shoes. Annie reached out and took one of his little hands in hers, wiggling it gently. "Hello, Toby."

For all intents and purposes this child was a stranger to her. Yet she had carried him inside her. She had given him life. But it was Sara and James who had shaped him into the little boy he was. Toby eventually giggled and in shyness pulled his hand back.

Eve put him on the floor and on wobbly legs he ran to his grandfather. Mick picked him up and set him on his knee.

"I swear, this boy gets bigger every day. He'll keep you on your toes this weekend, Annie."

She returned to helping Eve clear dishes, unable to stop from stealing glances at Toby now and then. "I'm looking forward to it."

"Grandma, may I be excused?"

Eve kissed the top of Caroline's head, ignoring the

cool tone of her voice. "Of course, dear. You and Luke can go watch television if you like."

The girl slid off the chair, pushing it in. "Are you coming, Toby?"

Instantly the boy wriggled down off his grandpa's knee and chased after his siblings as they disappeared into the living room.

In less than a minute, Annie heard the distinctive introduction for one of the more popular cartoon channels.

"I'm sorry about Caroline."

"Jared, it's okay. We both knew she was going to have a tough time with this."

Mick sat back in his chair and sipped his coffee. "We really appreciate what you're offering to do, Annie."

"I appreciate the chance Jared is giving me to have a family to care for and a place to belong."

"It must have been very lonely for you in the city," said Eve, coming to sit beside her husband, her eyes as soft as her smile. "I often wondered about you."

Annie couldn't remember a time when she hadn't been lonely. Even with Chris in her life she had felt alone—deep inside where nobody ever saw. "I learned a lot about inner strength and I learned to rely on my faith."

"Would you like to come to church on Sunday? Jared always brings the children."

Annie nodded. "I'd like that very much."

The older woman smiled back. "I think it's time for some homemade peach pie."

The rest of the evening was enjoyable for Jared. He

talked with his dad about crops while Annie helped his mother. In the back of his mind, worries persisted about Caroline but he hoped her fears could be worked through with time and love.

Annie fit in well here. His parents liked her, that was plain to see. Jared could imagine her back at the homestead, working in the kitchen, helping the children with their baths and homework.

He could imagine coming home every evening to the aroma of a home-cooked meal, without having to come in from the fields and throw something together.

His mother often came over and surprised him with something in the oven, and it usually lasted a few days but he had tried to be self-sufficient to a point.

When family services had started reviewing Caroline and Luke's placement, Jared had prayed for help. God had worked through Lewis and had found him Annie. He knew a lot of women these days wanted careers outside the home and if that made them happy he had no problem with it.

But it made him smile to think there were still some women out there who wanted to take care of a family. He knew some men dismissed it as an easy job. Jared had never made that mistake. Watching his mother raise two children, keep the house running smoothly and pay the bills while making ends meet had taught him about love and family.

On top of all that Eve had even gotten out in the fields and shearing shed at different times to help out where she could.

That was what life on the land was all about, he thought, watching Annie now. It was a partnership, a mutual goal and a willingness to work for that goal. He couldn't promise her the trappings of a real marriage but he could promise her the most important things.

Jared made the move to head off home a little before nine that evening. The kids, all still wide-awake, took their time saying goodbye.

"Caroline, you can sit in the back with the boys tonight."

The little girl paused on the way out the front door and turned to look at him.

"But Uncle Jared, I always sit up front with you."

Annie came up behind him. "Jared, I don't mind sitting in the back. This is just the first day. We'll take it slowly."

Jared didn't see the look of triumph Caroline gave Annie as she climbed into the front seat. The girl was letting her know that the first round had been played and won.

Annie wanted to pull her close and hug her, to let Caroline know it wasn't a contest—that no matter what happened after this weekend she would always come first with her uncle. But Annie knew her hugs would not be welcomed, not yet. It would be a slow process. Perhaps even a painful one for Caroline, if Jared agreed to the marriage.

Annie remembered what one of the nurses had told her the morning Toby was born. *You do what you are able with hope in your heart and leave the rest in the Lord's hands.*

Her heart squeezed tight the moment Toby came up

to her and held out his arms. He was ready to go in the car and he wanted her to put him there.

Annie reached down and caught him securely in her arms, hugging him close to her, inhaling that sweet baby smell that all little ones seemed to have. He was so soft in her arms, warm and yet quite heavy though he was an average size for his age. At one point he looked straight into her eyes and smiled.

Annie smoothed a hand over his forehead and gathered herself. "Let's get you in the truck, little man."

"Tuck!"

She smiled at him and tickled his belly as she settled him in the car seat. "Very good."

His giggle melted her heart. Soon they were headed home. Luke was talkative. Annie asked one question about his pets and the little boy had come alive, telling her all kinds of details.

Toby was content to play with the teddy bear he clutched in his hands and Caroline tuned the radio to a music station and stayed silent all the way home.

Back at the farm, Caroline and Luke were waiting on the porch for the adults by the time Annie managed to get Toby out. She set him on the ground and he made his way up the steps in what had to be record time. Jared unlocked the front door and they raced inside, heading straight for the laundry.

Moments later Annie heard the slamming of the back door.

"They always check the animals before bed. I think it would be okay if we skipped baths tonight."

Annie nodded. "They don't look any worse for wear and I noticed Luke yawning on the ride home."

"Caroline, too, though she tried hard not to let me see it."

"I really think it will be okay with her."

Jared wished he felt half as certain. "I just don't know when I should give in to her and where I need to draw the line."

"It's not an easy situation for anyone involved. We're all just finding our feet here and we have the benefit of being adults and understanding things a little more."

"Why don't you tuck her in tonight?" When Annie didn't reply he smiled. "I can come in with you if you'd like."

Annie took a deep breath. "Let me give it a whirl."

"Oh, before I forget." He reached onto the sideboard behind him. "This is the key to the red truck. You can use it to go between here and my parents' house."

"It was very kind of your mother to let me use her spare room." Annie was glad she didn't have to spend the night with him in this house, unchaperoned. With the child welfare people breathing down his neck the last thing Jared needed was even a hint of impropriety, and she was glad for other reasons. They were still virtually strangers, unsure of where this weekend would take them, what decisions would come or not come from it.

"Are you sure Toby's okay out there?"

"He doesn't like to go off the steps when it's dark out, even with the floodlight in the yard. He'll sit there and wait for them to finish feeding the animals." He motioned toward the stairs. "Let me show you the rest of the house."

He pointed out the kid's rooms as they passed each one and then he stopped and opened the last door on the right.

"This will be your room…if we go ahead with the marriage."

Annie didn't question why they would not sleep in the same room. This was not a marriage of love and passion. This was a marriage of commitment and friendship.

Everything in the room followed a lemon-and-white color scheme. The curtains matched the quilt on the bed and the rug in the middle of the floor looked so soft. The antique dresser, wardrobe and coordinating nightstand gave the room an old-world charm.

"You will always be free to make any changes to the room that you might like."

"Oh, I wouldn't want to change anything and if I ever did, I would ask you first."

He turned her to face him, his hands warm on her shoulders. "Annie, if we go ahead with this marriage, I don't want you to feel like you're a visitor."

Words escaped her, whether it was because he was standing so close or because he was looking at her as if he could see right through to her very soul.

"There are days when I walk into this house and expect to turn and see Sara in the kitchen cooking, or James outside working on some new project."

His hands slipped from her shoulders and he walked to the window. "I moved in here because it would have been too crowded with Mum and Dad…and in their will, Sara and James left the house and the farm to me. In turn they wanted me to someday pass it down to the children if any of them wanted to stay here and work it."

Annie walked up behind him and placed a comforting hand on his arm, a hand meant to reassure, but the touch had him turning to her. For a moment she forgot what she'd wanted to tell him.

"Don't take so much on yourself," she said quietly. "Let's just see how the next two days go."

He looked exhausted. It had been a long day.

"You're right."

"I'll try not to make a habit of it," she teased.

He cleared his throat and broke eye contact with her. "I'll go bring the kids in."

Jared left the room and Annie sat on the edge of the bed. She wondered what she would say to Caroline as she tucked her in.

Would the girl turn those cool eyes on her or, worse still, ignore the woman she saw as trying to take her uncle from her?

Annie couldn't make Caroline want her company or even her friendship. And in her heart she knew Caroline would more than likely push her away for a long time. But if she could win the girl's trust and acceptance in time then it would be worth all she had to do. If words didn't convince Caroline that her world was still safe and secure, then Annie would show her by actions.

She heard the kids come upstairs, giggling at something Jared said to them. With a silent prayer that she would do this right, Annie headed toward the door. Caroline's bedroom door was open. The girl was turning down her bed and laying her pyjamas out. Annie watched the precise, measured movements...so careful and controlled.

"Caroline?"

She turned at the sound of Annie's voice, her back stiffening slightly. "I'm getting ready for bed," she replied in that cool tone.

"May I help?"

"I don't need help." With that she crawled into the middle of her bed and hugged her pillow to her chest.

Annie came into the room. "Would it be okay if we talked for a few minutes?"

"Did Uncle Jared send you in here?"

"He asked me to check on you...make sure you had everything you needed for the night."

She looked at Annie as though she could see right through to her soul. "Your uncle loves you all so much...and if I come to live here...if we get married, it will be so you and Luke and Toby can stay together as a family."

"You won't be my mother," she said, her warning loud and clear. "You won't ever be a mother to me or my brothers."

Chapter Four

Annie felt for this little girl who was acting out in fear, not in spite or hate. "I never want to try and take your mother's place."

Tears shimmered on long dark lashes as Caroline looked toward the window. "Things will change now that you're here."

She spoke with such conviction that Annie longed to hug her but knew that would not be welcomed. All she could do was try to reassure her.

"Caroline, the only thing that is going to change will be that Uncle Jared doesn't have to do everything himself. I'll be here to help him."

She looked mutinously at Annie. "*I'm* the one who helps him."

Annie heard it in her voice, that being Jared's helper meant she was needed.

"I'd like to get ready for bed now."

"Good night, Caroline."

Annie heard her mumbled reply that could have been anything as she went out and closed the door. From the room down the hall, laughter filtered out.

She approached the room and caught sight of something moving very fast toward her. This "something" was giggling with delight.

"Annie, catch him…he's trying the bedtime escape." Jared laughed as he let Luke tackle him to the floor in a playful maneuver.

She scooped Toby up easily in her arms, swinging him around which made him laugh even harder. "Me go!"

"I don't think so, young man," she said. "I think it's bedtime for Toby."

Suddenly his smile turned into a frown. "No."

"Yes," came the decision from Jared. "Tomorrow is Saturday, plenty of time to run and play."

Jared pushed himself off the floor and deposited Luke on his bed. "Annie, would you change Toby into his pyjamas? They're at the end of his bed."

Toby wriggled and squirmed to the best of his ability but Annie held tight to him. "What are you…a worm?"

That irrepressible giggle bubbled up again and this time Annie found herself laughing with him. "Yuck."

"How about a little boy with way too much energy for this time of night?"

He clearly didn't understand but something told him that playtime was over and the adults were being serious now. His sigh was accompanied by a soft little pout.

"Wanna come fishing with us tomorrow, Annie?"

Jared pulled Luke's T-shirt over his face, which resulted in the boy mumbling the last of his invitation.

"That sounds like fun. Maybe we could pack some sandwiches and drinks."

"And cookies?"

"I'll see what I can do."

He turned his smile on his uncle. "I like her."

Jared kissed his forehead and deposited him in the bed. "I'm glad you do, mate."

That stamp of approval from Luke touched her.

When the boys were ready for sleep Jared kissed both of them and looked at Annie. "I'm going to check in on Caroline."

"Are you going to kiss us good night, Annie?"

She smoothed the light covers over Luke. "Would you like me to?"

His nod was emphatic. "Grandma kisses us 'night when we stay over there."

She leaned down and brushed her lips against his forehead.

"Don't forget Toby."

Annie walked over to where the child lay, his wide eyes taking in everything around him. He simply looked at her, as if memorizing her face.

She reached out and stroked the back of her hand down his cheek, let his long eyelashes brush her fingers, traced his sweet smile with one trembling finger.

This was something she never thought she would get to do, kiss her son good-night. "Sleep tight, little man." She leaned down and brushed a kiss against his forehead.

"See you in the morning, boys." She slipped out of the room and closed the door quietly behind her. When she turned, Jared was standing right there.

"They're settled for the night."

"Caroline, too." Then he pulled a key from his pocket. "This is for the front door so you can come and go as you like."

Annie took it. In such a small way that key made her situation so much more real. "Thanks."

"I need some coffee. You interested?"

Annie screwed up her nose a little. "I don't drink coffee but I'll have a cup of tea with you."

"After you," he said, motioning for her to lead the way downstairs. Once they were in the kitchen she decided now was as good a time as any to learn where things were.

"Sit down and let me see if I can navigate this on my own."

He smiled but did as she said. In the cabinet above the coffeemaker she found mugs. In the large walk-in pantry she found coffee, filters, teabags and sugar. She busied herself trying not to feel like an interloper in Sara's kitchen.

"How was Caroline with you tonight?"

Jared rubbed the back of his neck. "Stony silence. I really believe she's thinking about it all, though."

Annie prayed time would banish Caroline's fears. "So what time will we be going fishing?"

"Late in the afternoon is best. I've morning chores to do, Luke and Caroline have the animal houses to clean and I think we need a load of laundry."

"If you prefer you can write me a list."

"No, that makes you seem like hired help and I don't want you to feel that way. I'll let you take care of the indoor stuff this weekend…if you don't mind."

"Mind?" She laughed as the last of the coffee brewed. "I'd love to try and find my way, see if I can get into a routine…I just don't want you to feel like I'm taking over."

Jared was quiet until she set coffee in front of him and sat down at the table with a cup of tea for herself. "Annie, I know you'll feel a little strange at first but don't be afraid to do things."

Annie sipped her tea. "What time do you usually get up for breakfast on the weekends?"

"Same time as during the week. I'm in the kitchen by about five-thirty…sometimes six depending on what the weather is like and what I have on the agenda for the day. Never any later than six though."

Six in the morning! Well, this was the country. The day started as the sun was breaking, sometimes before.

"On Sundays I feed the animals and do the milking but that's about it for outside chores," he told her. "We get ready for church after breakfast and then we have lunch either here or with Mum and Dad. Then I catch up on the accounts and farm records in the afternoon."

"Do you manage the household accounts on computer?"

"I don't but we have the software to do it." He thought for a moment then added. "If we make this a permanent thing, would you like to take over the budgeting and accounts for the house?"

Annie smiled. "I'd love to." She inquired as to what software he had and was delighted to learn it was the same one she had used at the restaurant.

"He had you doing the books?"

"Nobody else wanted to do them and he wasn't very good at numbers. At first I didn't know a whole lot about it, but I read the manuals and I'd go in and play around with it on my days off. After a month or so I was able to save him money and show him how the business could be more efficient."

"The computer is in the study, just off the living room. Feel free to use it anytime."

They fell into a calm silence, neither feeling compelled to rush headlong into conversation just to fill it. Finally Annie had a question.

"What do you all like for breakfast?"

"The kids make up their minds when they reach the table. Sometimes it's cereal, sometimes toast. On the odd occasion they'll ask for pancakes, and once I tried French toast because they made it in Caroline's class at school."

"How did it turn out?"

"Burnt beyond recognition," he confessed, a soft smile on his face. "Sara has cookbooks on one of the shelves in the pantry. I doubt there's anything you can't find."

He took a sip of coffee. "I think today went well, all things considered."

Annie had to agree. "I'm looking forward to the weekend." She did say it, but she knew come Monday she would be hoping to hear his decision.

"I'm going to head up to bed," he said, stifling a yawn. "I've been up since five. You're okay to get back to the farm? I'll drive you if you want me to."

"It's a straight shot down the road. I won't get lost. You need your sleep."

He pushed to his feet. "You can leave the cups in the sink. I'll do them in the morning. What time will you be here tomorrow?"

Annie took the cups from the table and deposited them in the sink. "I'll be here in time to cook your breakfast. This is a trial run—I'd better get used to your schedule."

He seemed about to say something then shook his head, exhausted. "Thanks for the coffee…you made it just right."

"I'm glad you enjoyed it."

He bid her good-night and went upstairs. She listened to the sound of his footsteps retreating. "I've passed my first day," she said quietly to the silent room. "Please Lord, help me make tomorrow a good day for all of us."

Upstairs, Jared lay in bed listening to the sound of Annie cleaning up in the kitchen, moving chairs. He heard the front door close and click to lock.

In moments the truck was fired up and disappearing into the distance.

He didn't want to pressure her into thinking she had to want this. Twenty-one was such a young age. When he was that age all he'd thought about was football, women and cars.

Annie seemed so grounded, so ready to accept the awesome responsibility he was asking her to take on. Whatever had happened in her past, it hadn't destroyed her. It had made her stronger.

As he drifted into sleep, Jared said a silent prayer, for the future, for all of them. He prayed that things would go well this weekend and Annie would feel she had a place here.

Annie made it out to the farm the next morning before anyone was awake. She had showered and dressed as quietly as she could so as not to wake Eve and Mick.

She was dressed in jeans and a button-front blouse of white eyelet. Her hair was pulled back into a ponytail. The sandals on her feet made a muffled noise on the floor of the hallway as she let herself in the front door.

She set the table, slowly discovering where things were, trying not to think about the restless night she'd had. That little voice inside had kept nagging at her about telling Jared the truth. It had kept reminding her of all the opportunities she'd had to tell him. Annie had tried hard to ignore it.

She had instead tried to concentrate on the most important part of her being here…the children. Last night, seeing Toby for the first time wasn't as tough as she'd expected.

Seeing him forced a realization on her. If Jared asked her to marry him and if she said yes, she would never be able to tell anyone that Toby was her son.

Annie was determined not to show favoritism. She would give them all the same love and attention equally.

"Good morning."

Annie swung around at the sound of Jared's voice. He came walking into the kitchen, his shirt not yet tucked into his jeans, work boots in one hand, till he dropped them on the floor beside his chair.

He began rolling up his shirtsleeves and Annie realized what a thoroughly masculine thing it was…inconsequential in the course of a day but a little thing she noticed this morning. He sat down on a chair at the table, turning to put his boots on.

"I opened the window so I could hear the sounds of the morning."

He looked at her with a thoughtful expression, then he smiled. "You know, I guess for those of us who hear it every day it just becomes another part of country life. But you haven't heard it in so long."

"It's beautiful. There is no sound I'm sure, like that of the Australian bush waking up each morning." She moved away from the window and poured him a cup of freshly brewed coffee.

"I made it just like last night. What would you like for breakfast?"

"Eggs would be good."

"How do you have them?"

He smiled. "Scrambled with cheese and onion."

She bestowed on him a smile that was as innocent and as warm as she was. "I worked the breakfast shift a few times and filled in for the cook on more than one occasion. My eggs never killed anyone."

"That's good to know."

Jared watched as she moved around the kitchen, curious about this woman. He had never in his life known a woman as complex and intriguing, yet one who seemed happy with the smallest things in life.

Annie took pride in putting the plate of eggs before him when they were done. "I used a little cream. It makes them fluffier…at least, that's the theory."

Jared had eaten at least three mouthfuls before he could finally manage a verdict. "Annie, this is great."

Behind her the toaster tinged. She came back to the table with four slices of toast smothered with butter.

"On the off chance that we decide not to get married. I may hire you on as our cook."

Before he could ask she had refilled his coffee mug. "As a cook, I don't come cheap and I expect good tips."

He was chuckling at her reply when Luke ambled in, one hand scratching his head, the other stifling a yawn. He still wore his pyjamas.

"Morning, mate."

Still not properly awake, Luke waved at his uncle as he sat down at the table. "Can I have cereal, please?"

"Sure." Annie didn't know what to choose from the pantry. There staring back at her were four boxes of cereal, each one different, each box more colorful.

She felt Jared behind her before his warm breath

grazed her ear. Annie closed her eyes and tried not to feel the awareness that tore a path through her.

"You'll find he tends to like whichever one has some free toy in the box or one of those superhero stories on the back."

By the time he moved away to put his plate in the sink, Annie was wiping her sweaty palm on her jeans. He hadn't meant it to be an intimate gesture…Jared wasn't like that. So why had it seemed so cozy…so personal? He didn't seem affected at all by the innocent encounter as he sat back down at the table.

Luke had already gotten the milk from the refrigerator and carried it back to the table. He was happily munching on purple-and-green rings of some sugar coated cereal when his sister came into the kitchen.

"Good morning, Caroline."

She threw Annie a glance. "Morning."

"Hey, Possum. Luke wants to go fishing today."

Caroline busied herself getting a bowl, a spoon and another brand of cereal before coming back to the table. She settled in a chair opposite her uncle.

"I'd like to go play with Michelle today."

Jared took a deep breath and decided to at least attempt to handle this situation better than those of the last few days.

"You've got the animal houses to clean and then I thought we could all have a picnic and go fishing at the river."

"After I do the houses, will you call Michelle's mum and ask if I can come over?"

Jared shrugged. "Okay, if that's what you want." Before Caroline could look too comfortable that she had gotten her own way, he added, "We'll pick you up on the way to the river. That way you'll get to do both."

Caroline looked at him as if he had just betrayed her and it hurt Jared.

"I'll go see if Toby is awake." Annie quietly left the room.

"Caroline, no matter how hard you try not to like Annie, she's still going to be nice to you."

"I just don't want to go fishing."

Luke looked surprised. "But you love fishing."

"I don't feel like going today."

"You mean you don't want to spend time with Annie." She didn't answer Jared but her look told him he was right. "I thought you would at least give her a chance. She doesn't want to take anything away from you, she just wants to be your friend."

Caroline let out a frustrated sigh. "Fine. I'll go fishing."

Jared smiled and reached out to brush a strand of hair from her face. "Thank you."

As she looked back to her cereal bowl Jared felt he'd made great strides with that one concession on her part.

"Are you part worm or part contortionist?"

Trying to dress Toby had been one giggle after another from him.

"Let's go get you some breakfast."

She set him on his feet and took his hand. "'Kay."

Annie smiled to herself as she led Toby down the hall and carefully down each step. He took his time and she didn't mind at all.

Toby jumped down the last step and ran ahead into the kitchen. Annie paused and looked up at the photos on the wall.

She stared at Sara's photograph and a strange, though warm feeling filled her. "I wish I could have told him. But your brother just would not understand…not like you did."

And then, it was as if the other woman reached out in some way and laid a hand on her shoulder…to let her know it was all right.

A peace filled Annie and her voice was whisper soft. "I'll take care of them all for you, Sara…I promise."

"You can pet Oscar if you'd like."

Annie pegged the last of Jared's shirts on the line and looked down at Luke and the guinea pig he held in his hand. Gingerly she ran her hand over the quivering little ball of chocolate-brown fur. "Nice to meet you, Oscar."

"I can bring his family up for you to meet."

"Ah, that's okay, Luke…I'm sure we'll meet sooner or later."

He shrugged and ran off, Oscar clutched tightly to his little chest. Earlier that day he had introduced her to the cats, Tabby, Mouser and Fluffy.

The only worrying thing to the whole lovable picture was that Fluffy had not an ounce of fur on her anywhere.

Annie wasn't sure what breed she was but her name certainly seemed ironic.

Toby was amusing himself in the sandpit, Murphy sitting close by watching him. The boys had been playing outside since lunchtime. Caroline was spending a few hours with her friend and Jared was in the shed working on the engine of an old blue truck.

Annie picked up the basket and carried it back into the house. This was what her days would be like if Jared agreed to the marriage: routine household chores, spending time with the children, being in their lives and hopefully making a difference.

She was cutting up sandwiches, preparing to pack the picnic hamper, when Jared came into the house, pausing to rinse his hands and drying them on the clean hand towel she passed him.

"Thanks. How long until you're ready?"

"As soon as I finish putting the goodies in here."

He put the towel back on the rack, snatched a sandwich from the pile and shot her a smile. "I'll go put the fishing gear in the truck."

Annie went to the back door and called the boys in. They were a little grubby but happy, with that rosy cheeked look of healthy children. It was especially heartwarming to watch Toby mimic his brother, his tiny little legs pumping as he raced headlong to catch up at times.

With the boys sitting at the table a few minutes later, both content to drink cool ice water and watch her, Annie finished packing the hamper, throwing in extra juice boxes and napkins.

By the time she had assured herself she had everything they could possibly need, Jared came back into the kitchen.

"I'll carry this." He took the hamper with an ease that shouldn't have surprised her. "Are we ready?"

The boys shouted their answers and charged after their uncle and out the door. Annie wiped her hands on the dishtowel before switching off the light and following them.

She couldn't think of a nicer way to spend a Saturday afternoon. Hopefully there would be many more like it in the future.

"If it's okay with you, I'm going to take an hour for myself tomorrow." Annie smoothed the blanket on which she was sitting.

They had been at the river for almost two hours. Caroline was laughing and smiling and having fun with her brothers but each time her eyes met with Annie's, a guarded expression took the smile away and dimmed the light in her eyes.

Jared looked up from rigging his fishing pole, a wary look on his face. "If it's all been overwhelming, I'm sorry."

Annie smiled and closed the picnic hamper. "Nothing about you or the children is overwhelming. I want to go over and see what's left of my old house."

"Annie, there's nothing but a couple of walls and the chimney still standing."

"I heard there was a fire. I knew there couldn't have

been much left but I need to close that part of my life. I wish I could explain it but I can't." She shrugged. "I was just so angry when I left here. I need to make peace."

He turned and looked down to where the children sat high up on the riverbank and out of harm's way. "I think I understand. Sometimes unfinished business just seems to want to drag you back."

"You, too?" He nodded. "Were you ever able to go back and finish it?"

"I thought about it a time or two…but I know there wouldn't be any point. I chose my life and it's right here in front of me." He looked from the children back to her. "I think it's a pretty good life."

Then why, she wondered, *did it sound like something was missing? Lord, please help Jared find the peace his soul needs.*

"My worm wriggled off."

Both adults realized they had been so caught up in the conversation, neither had seen Luke amble up the hill.

"He might have been snatched by a fish," Jared suggested, reaching into the pail and dragging out another big fat worm.

Luke shook his head. "Nah, he fell off 'cause I didn't feel any tugging on my line." He looked up Annie. "Could I have another cookie, please?"

She handed him the sandwich bag. "Take them down and share them with the others."

He grinned as he took his newly baited pole and went back down the bank.

"Thank you for today." Jared handed her a fishing pole he had finished rigging. "I know Caroline's attitude is probably a damper but it means a lot to me and the boys."

Annie smiled. "You're welcome, and thank you for inviting me to be a part of this."

He pushed to his feet and held out his hand to her.

"Come on, let's go see if you're as good a fisherman as you are in the kitchen."

Laughing, she let him pull her to stand and followed him.

Later that evening the children watched one of their favorite movies in the living room and Annie sat in front of the computer, slowly figuring out the accounting software.

Jared had insisted on cleaning up in the kitchen after dinner. It hadn't been much. They were all still stuffed from the picnic.

"I brought you a cup of tea."

Annie looked up as Jared came into the study with two mugs. He handed one to her and came around to stand behind her.

"This software came with the computer. Do you think it's something you'll be able to use?"

"It's a newer version of the one I used before, but not that different. Once I see the receipts you have, I can set up folders for your different accounts, work out a budget if you'd like one and tell you how much you're spending on both farm items and household things."

"Amazing," said Jared, just watching her click here

or tap on a key there and move through programs like a pro. She was a revelation in so many ways. Everything he had seen so far—her rapport with the children, her patience with Caroline and her willingness to pitch in and be part of the life he had here—all led him to one conclusion.

Jared knew there was a possibility she might change her mind about liking it here so much, but instinct told him if he asked her to stay, she would.

"What's on the agenda for tomorrow?" She shut down the computer before turning to face him.

"Church."

The smile she gave him was not feigned and that touched him. "I guess the people of the town will be curious as to why I'm back and why I'm with your family."

"They'll find out soon enough." He held out his hand. "Let's go finish watching the movie with the kids."

Annie took his hand and once again felt little pinpricks of awareness. She'd felt them today, too. They weren't intimidating, but hinted at aspects of their relationship she had tried not to dwell on.

The moment they sat down on the couch Luke got up from his position on the floor and came to sit on his uncle's knee, curling into the broad chest.

Toby, copying what his big brother did, came over to the couch and, seeing Jared's lap occupied, climbed up and perched himself on Annie.

"I'm glad he's taken to you so well."

Annie couldn't tell him how wonderful it was to her,

she couldn't tell him just what the moments with Toby meant to her. If she told him, this would all end. It hurt to keep the truth bottled inside.

Toby eventually drifted off to sleep, curling into Annie's chest, his thumb in his mouth, his breathing soft and even.

Jared felt his breath stall when he looked over at the pair. It looked so natural, the child sleeping peacefully, the woman holding him like he belonged in her arms. He wondered if she even realized that her fingers smoothed softly over his tiny head, or that now and again she bestowed the smallest of kisses in his hair.

Annie Dawson seemed tailor-made to fit into all their lives. Tomorrow at church, Jared would have a lot to be thankful for.

Annie drove with Jared's parents to church the next day. How she'd agonized over what to wear this morning, wanting to look just right! Finally she'd settled on a pale lavender summer dress, with short sleeves and a hemline that brushed her calves. It fitted her slender shape except where the skirt billowed and fell softly around her legs. She had her hair rolled and swept up off her neck, secured with pins.

Jared looked very handsome today dressed in a shirt and tie, crisply pressed trousers and black dress shoes. If it was possible he looked even more masculine than usual.

Mick placed a fatherly arm around her shoulder and gave her a gentle squeeze, but once the children rushed at him she moved away and walked to stand beside Jared.

It hadn't escaped Jared's notice that people were casting glances in their direction. He saw the recognition on some people's faces, saw some grasp for an old memory of the pretty woman with red hair and smiling eyes.

She looked especially beautiful today. She constantly surprised him, amazing him at every turn, making him shake his head and wonder how he could have found someone so perfect for his world, for the children.

"Annie Dawson?"

Annie braced herself as she turned toward the voice that had questioningly called her name. She came face to face with a girl who had saved her a seat on the school bus many times, a girl she had always liked.

"Susie Cooper!"

The woman chuckled, hands resting on the swell of her belly. "Susie Peters now. I married Danny. Hi, Jared."

"Susie."

"How is Danny?" Annie enquired.

"He's fine. That's him over there trying to keep an eye on the twins."

She remembered Danny as short and round but the man who walked toward them now, his eyes on his wife, had grown tall and slender. He greeted Jared and shook his hand.

"Sweetheart, you remember Annie Dawson from Rivers Road?"

Suddenly a smile broke out on his cheerful face. "Sure do. How are you? Moving back to town or just visiting?"

"I'm fine and still deciding on the moving back part." She didn't know what else to say. "How long until the new addition?"

Susie sighed. "Nine weeks and I'm so ready you couldn't imagine."

Annie bit back the response that hovered on her tongue. She could imagine all too well. "And you have twin boys already?"

"Yep, but the doctor tells me this time there's only one."

Annie touched the woman's arm. "It was lovely seeing you both again and good luck."

Susie beamed. "Thanks. Come on Danny, we'd better head on in and get a seat. Boys, time to go in."

Jared scooped Toby into his arms and Luke slipped his hand into Annie's as they made their way into the church with Jared's parents.

Annie felt like a bug under a microscope as they entered the church. They chose a row in the middle, and even when everyone was settled she knew people had recognized her or were trying to place her face. Jared looked over at her and without saying a word he took her hand and gave it a gentle squeeze. Then he smiled and took her breath away.

She was still reeling from the effects of that smile when a gentle hand touched her shoulder.

"Sweet Annie."

The minister who stood in front of her now was as familiar to her as anyone. "Reverend Kane. How lovely to see you again."

"And you, my dear. Jared, good to see you." He looked back to Annie. "We've missed you. Maybe you've come home to stay?"

He moved away to greet Mick and Eve farther up in the pew before taking his place at the front of the church and greeting the congregation.

"I had a sermon prepared for this morning but today I'm going to talk about going home," he said. "Whether it is to our own past or the Lord's family, nobody should ever feel they couldn't go home again."

Chapter Five

As Jared listened to the sermon, he took every word to heart. He wished sometimes that he could go home, that he could confront his past and make peace with whatever he was able to.

This hadn't been his life plan but he'd long ago come to realize that life rarely worked out to anyone's specifications. He had learned to follow the Lord's plan for his life, not his own. Now he expected the unexpected and rolled with the punches.

Annie's hand felt soft and warm in his and at one point, Jared closed his eyes and let the feeling of that touch, the words of the sermon, just soak into him.

When it was over they filed out with the rest of the congregation. Many more people came up and said hello to Annie. She was gracious with them all, though Jared recalled some of them had not been very charitable at one time to the quiet little girl or her mother.

With the children back in the truck they followed Mick and Eve to their house for a Sunday lunch of roast chicken and vegetables.

For Annie the day seemed to go too fast. Lunch was a happy occasion. Though Caroline didn't say a word to Annie, the little girl was boisterous with the other adults and with her brothers. It occurred to Annie that maybe she was happy because this evening Jared was taking her home. She had a feeling she would be coming back in the very near future.

Later that afternoon Jared kept the children at the house and Annie drove the truck out to Rivers Road. As what was left of her old house came into view, a burning sensation began in the pit of her stomach.

She didn't know if it was fear. She wasn't sure how much of those feelings inside her were bad memories and how much was a longing for things to have been different.

She pulled the truck up the driveway and stopped, got out and gingerly made her way through the now half-fallen gate.

Her mother had never known how she dreaded coming home from school through this gate each day, for it was a rare occurrence that her mother hadn't been passed out inside.

Jared was right, nothing but two walls and the chimney stack remained—that and her memories. She had cried many nights trying to wake her mother up, sometimes fearing she was dead. She'd hated people coming to the door, looking at her with eyes filled with a pity that more often than not changed to scorn when her mother came into view.

Annie's mother had never accepted handouts from anyone, not even the ladies from the church. She'd fought to keep her daughter even when she hadn't really wanted her. To Annie it seemed that her mother didn't want her to have anything better, that if *she* had to suffer, then she would make sure her child suffered with her.

A shiver skittered up her spine as her mother's voice came back to her. The names had hardened her. The accusations of a life ruined because of her had made Annie resilient enough to survive.

It had taken a long time—and a great deal of faith—before she had found it in herself to believe that she hadn't ruined her mother's life by being born. Her mother had let alcohol do that long before.

"Thank you, Lord, for bringing me so far from this house, from that awful time," she prayed quietly.

As she turned to go, Annie felt as though she had crossed an important bridge. She didn't want to go back now that she had made peace with the part of her past that had haunted her.

She got into the truck and started it, putting it in gear before rolling back out of the driveway. As she drove away, leaving it in a cloud of dust in her rearview mirror a certainty once again filled her heart.

The guilt would eat her up inside, but if Jared asked her to marry him she was going to say yes.

* * *

"It seems like the weekend has just flown by." Jared came to sit beside her in the back porch chairs that afternoon.

The children played on the trampoline, their giggles and voices raised in joy and happiness filling the sun-kissed day.

"I've enjoyed it."

"So have I. More importantly, you've made my decision easier."

Annie felt silly holding her breath but she couldn't help it. She swallowed a lump that had formed in her throat.

"Would you marry me?" His voice was steady and sure, his tone calm and quiet. "Would you live here and help me make a life for the children?"

"Yes."

He smiled. "That was a quick answer."

"I love the children and I love this place. This is something important I can do with my life. I was so lonely in the city and my life seemed to have no purpose."

She looked across at the children. "Sara was my friend. I want to do this for her. But are *you* sure, Jared?"

"Yes. As long as you're absolutely certain you can live with the terms. I'm not offering you love and romance. I can't even promise you that those feelings will come in time."

Annie was grateful for his honesty. "I understand. You don't have to explain."

"Yes, I do. I'm asking you to accept a marriage proposal knowing that you may never feel your husband's lips on yours in passion. Knowing that you may live the rest of your life and never have the physical part of marriage that most people take for granted or come to see as a chore."

He paused and searched her face. "You're a beautiful young woman, Annie, and you have the same feelings and emotions as any other."

She actually managed a smile and sat back in the porch chair shaking her head. "Jared, I lost someone close to me a while back so I'm not rushing to find romance or intimacy."

"I'm sorry." He tried to hide his surprise, wondering just how close she had been to this person.

Annie shrugged. "He's in a wonderful place and the people whose lives he touched are better for it."

Jared wanted to be happy that she'd had a special love in her life, but knowing about it caused him to wonder things he had no business knowing.

"I believe we can build a life together as companions and friends." And knowing she wasn't looking for love made it that much easier to ask her.

Annie couldn't look away from those eyes. "I believe it, too. We'll just have to be patient with Caroline until she decides to accept me."

Jared squeezed her hand. "I can't offer you the things a woman should be offered by a man proposing marriage to her. But you have my respect and my support."

He folded her fingers beneath his. "I'll protect you

and keep you safe. I'll provide well for you and the children and I'll work hard. I can promise you laughter and happy times, some hard times perhaps, but I'll try to keep them to a minimum."

He took a deep breath. "That is all I have to give."

Annie smiled, touched by his words and his honesty. "It's more than a lot of people ever have. It will be enough."

Once again, in the midst of this perfect afternoon Annie felt guilt well inside her. Jared deserved to know the truth but she couldn't bring herself to tell him.

"My promise to you is that I will be here to share the load with you. I'll be here when you get home in the evening and you can tell me about your day."

"That sounds nice."

"I'll be the best mother I can be to the children."

He sat back in his chair and closed his eyes, not saying anything for several moments. When he looked back at her there was a peace in his expression that she hadn't seen before.

"Then it's settled?"

"Yes."

And just like that her future was decided, with a man who was as honest as he was hardworking, a man who had left her with no expectations of anything but what they had found this weekend.

Annie Dawson was getting married. The Lord certainly did work in mysterious ways, she thought as she looked at the finger that would soon bear Jared's ring.

They told the children a short while later. Seated

around the kitchen table, Toby on Jared's knee, the children snacked on watermelon slices as their uncle broke the news.

"Does that mean you'll be here forever and ever?" Luke's question was filled with such innocence, yet how could she promise him that?

"I'll be here as long as I'm able. Probably until you're an old man."

His eyes grew wide. "That long? Wow."

Caroline sat stone-faced, no smile, just a harsh acceptance in her expression. "It means Uncle Jared won't need us as much now to help him with stuff."

Luke took her words to heart and looked genuinely worried. Jared cast her a stern look and intervened. "It means no such thing. Annie and I are counting on help from all of you. That is what a family does and that is what we will be…a family."

Luke shot his sister a "so there" smile and went back to chomping on his watermelon.

"May I be excused?" Caroline pushed her plate away.

Jared sighed. "Yes, you may. I want you to pack your bag for a stay at Grandma's tonight."

"You're going away?" It was an accusation.

"I'm taking Annie back to pick up her things and put everything in order and I need to see Uncle Lewis."

Caroline was silent for a moment then asked, "Can we go with you?"

Jared was ready to give a clear objection but something stopped him, be it the look in his niece's eyes or the tone of her voice.

Could it be bothering her, the fact that he was going away and leaving them? He'd had a few meetings in the city with Lewis and then those with the Department of Family Services.

"Annie, would you mind if the kids came with us?"

Her smile was the same one he'd come to look for these past few days. "Not at all."

In fact, Annie thought it a very good idea. Including the children in what was happening around them and to their world was bound to make the changes a little less traumatic.

"If we can get our overnight bags packed I'll go call Lewis and tell him we're on our way."

Caroline blessed him with a smile as she hugged him quickly and ran out the door, pounding up the stairs. Annie took Toby's hand when Jared placed him on the floor and Luke followed her upstairs.

Lewis answered his phone on the second ring. He offered his congratulations when Jared told him about the impending marriage.

"Do you feel like being invaded?"

His chuckle was filled with affection. "You're bringing the munchkins?"

"Yeah. Caroline wanted to come and since she's having a hard time dealing with all these changes I thought it might help her not to feel left out."

"I'll get Harriet to make up the spare rooms."

"Thanks, mate."

"Annie's a good person, Jared. She'll be good for the kids...and for you." Before Jared could interrupt and remind his friend that it was not a conventional marriage, Lewis spoke again. "There's the other line…I have to go.

See you in a few hours."

He hung up the telephone and the sound of laughter reached his ears. He heard Annie's voice, though he couldn't make out what she was saying.

This was all he knew to do, to keep Sara's family together. He realized the gravity of the future ahead of him. Jared didn't deny to himself that a little of what he felt was fear. It was a big commitment for him, though one he hadn't even thought twice about making.

He would have a responsibility to Annie, as well. He knew she would work as hard as him to give the children what they needed.

"We're just about ready."

He looked up at the sound of her voice to see Annie standing in the doorway to the study. "The kids are just feeding and watering their animals."

Jared got to his feet. "I'll go pack a bag and then we can go. We'll swing by Mum and Dad's place on the way out of town."

When they arrived twenty minutes later, his parents were pleased about the news of the marriage, yet Annie sensed some apprehension.

Eve hugged her warmly nonetheless when Jared told them. "I know you'll be a wonderful addition to our family."

Annie wanted to be close to this woman and to have a relationship with her like she was never able to have with her own mother. "Thank you. I'll do my best for Jared and the children."

The answering smile was soft and warm. "Your best is going to be just fine."

"Eve, I was wondering if you would help me with the wedding preparations. I'd prefer something small and family oriented, but I've never planned anything like this before."

Eve actually had to blink back tears, but not before Annie saw them glistening briefly on her eyelashes. "I would love to help. We'll get right to it as soon as you get back and settle in."

Jared accepted his father's handshake. "Congratulations, son."

"Thanks, Dad. I know this is the right thing to do."

Mick nodded. "We support your decision."

Eve was next to hug her son, while Mick moved to chat with the children in the truck. "I'll call the school tomorrow morning and explain to Mrs. Henderson about them being absent."

Jared smiled. "Thanks."

"You'd better get going and cover as many miles as you can before nightfall."

Jared knew his mother hated him traveling at night. Sara and James had been traveling at night when their accident happened.

"I promise I'll be careful."

Eve smiled, though worry lingered in her eyes. "Be very sure that you do."

She watched them drive off, waved to her grandchildren and hugged her husband. "She's a very special young woman."

Mick put his arm around her, squeezing her shoulders gently. "Yes, she is. I think Annie is going to change our son's life more than he realizes."

"You need to decide if you'd like an outfit specially made for the day or if you'd like to buy something off the rack."

Annie folded the last load of laundry on the kitchen table as Eve looked over the list they had made. Toby was taking his afternoon nap upstairs and Jared was out in one of the paddocks checking for holes in their fences.

She'd been here almost a week now, already settling into a simple and contentment-filled routine. This day found her sitting in Eve's kitchen, discussing the upcoming wedding and the dress she would wear. "I'd like something old-fashioned if I could find it."

Though she had never really expected to get married, the little girl in her had always dreamed of the fairy-tale gown.

Eve sipped her coffee. "You have excellent taste. A figure like yours and that gorgeous hair would look wonderful in a Victorian style."

Annie blushed, but accepted the compliment. "Where would we find something like that?"

"Maggie's Attic on Main Street. She may have something in her back rooms. That poor woman always has too much merchandise to put out at one time."

"We could go tomorrow once I drop the kids off at school. I could come by and pick you up."

"That sounds great. If you like, Toby can stay with Mick. He'd love the company," she said. "Those children help to keep him young."

"I'm sure Toby would love that."

Eve looked at the kitchen wall clock. "I'd best be heading on home to see about dinner."

"I'm going to put this laundry away then go pick the kids up from school."

Eve hugged her. "I am so very glad my son brought you back into our lives and I'm even happier that he got you to stay."

Annie instinctively hugged her back, savoring warmth that she had always wanted to know, wanted to feel. This woman was so different from her mother and yet she knew they would be close. Even in the worst times with her own mother, Annie had always felt a flicker of hope in her heart that Sylvia would somehow come to love her. She had struggled these past few years with forgiveness. The Lord spoke often of forgiveness in His teachings, but Annie knew it was something she had to find within herself.

She left a note on the refrigerator for Jared telling him where she was going and then went upstairs to wake Toby.

He came awake easily, one lasting yawn before his bright little eyes and cheeky smile surfaced. His smile was huge when she told him where they were going.

That smile gave in to shrieks of delight when she

pulled the four-wheel-drive truck up outside the school. Luke spotted her first and made his way quickly through the throng of children.

He hopped into the back seat and put his belt on. "Hi, Annie."

"Did you have a good day?"

He shook his head. "I got reading homework."

"I'll help you if you like."

Just then the front door opened and Caroline put her backpack on the floor. She was about to get in when she hesitated. "Should I sit in the back?"

Annie smiled. "Of course not. When it's just the four of us in the car, I'd love it if you would sit up front with me."

Caroline gave no indication of what she was thinking, just climbed in and settled into the seat, clicking her belt.

Annie pulled out of the parking lot and onto the road that would lead them through town and eventually home.

"Actually, I wanted to know if you'd like to come shopping with me and Grandma on Saturday."

Caroline cast a quiet glance at her. "Shopping for what?"

"I'd like to find you a dress for the wedding. I was hoping you would be my junior bridesmaid and Luke and Toby would be ring bearers."

She'd discussed it with Jared and he had liked the idea. She didn't want the children to feel left out in any way and weddings were always more special when children took part.

"I'll wear one of the dresses Mummy made for me." She stared straight ahead, hands folded in her lap.

Annie didn't pressure her. "I think that sounds nice." She couldn't help the feeling that Caroline was slipping further and further away from her.

She hadn't expected it would be easy; she just hadn't figured the little girl would be so determined not to like her. The daily belligerence and the dark glaring silences had subsided since their night spent in the city with Lewis. She was respectful now, and polite, but only spoke when Annie spoke directly to her and kept her distance.

"Dinner was wonderful, Annie."

She was stacking the dishes after putting away the remainder of the beef casserole she'd prepared. "I'm glad you liked it."

Annie expected him to excuse himself and leave the room, but instead he leaned against the cook top and watched her go from table to sink.

"So you're going shopping with Mum tomorrow?"

Annie was pleased just to have something to talk about…anything was better than him staring at her in silence.

"Yes. She's positive we can find something that suits me."

This time when she passed him, he stopped her with a hand on her shoulder. Annie slowly turned to look at him, keeping a tight grip on the glasses in her hands. She swallowed the sudden dryness in her mouth. He was, hands down, the most handsome man she'd ever met. And the kindest, gentlest person she'd ever known.

"Are you wearing your hair up or down for the ceremony?"

His voice was low, an intensity to it that she hadn't heard before. "I hadn't really decided."

"Do something for me?" When she didn't answer, he smiled. "Wear it down."

After a few stunned, electrically charged moments, she frowned. "Why?"

He shrugged, letting his hand drop from her shoulder. "Because your hair is beautiful."

He emptied what was left of his coffee down the sink and gave her one last look before heading into the living room.

When he was gone, Annie sagged back against the kitchen counter. After he had spelled out to her what kind of marriage they were going to have, why was he indulging in these intimate moments that left her breathless?

She could fall in love with Jared far too easily if she allowed it. Then what would she do? Pine for a man who would never love her?

She hadn't let anyone into her heart since Chris, and after his death she'd figured there had been enough hurt in her life without inviting it in again.

Falling in love with Jared Campbell would mean hurt with a capital H. Yet even as she told herself this moment could never happen again, she knew in her heart that she would wear her hair down.

She would do it because even though her marriage to Jared would not include anything physical, just the look in his eyes when he'd asked her to do that for him was one she could live on forever.

It was the only wedding she would ever have and unconventional or not, she wanted to look her best. She wanted him to notice her on that special day, though she was not about to question why she wanted that.

She mentally laid down guidelines for their relationship while she methodically cleaned every inch of the kitchen and straightened everything but the curtains.

Finally she realized she couldn't put it off forever. Walking into the living room, she smiled at a sight that had become familiar to her in just the week since she'd moved in.

Toby played with his trucks in front of the television, now and then looking up, captivated by the children's video that was playing.

Caroline sat at the small table in the corner, her face a study in concentration. She took her schoolwork very seriously and at the moment Jared was explaining something to her and she was giving him her full attention.

Luke came to her as she sat down on the couch. "I hate reading." He climbed up beside her and put the book in her lap.

"Books can take you on amazing adventures," she said, seeing his frown. She put her arm around him and settled back. "You can go searching for buried treasure and be a pirate. You can find giants in other lands or ride camels in the desert. If you open a book it will take you anywhere."

He thought for a moment. "But the words are hard to learn."

"That's why you practice, a little every night. Then when your teacher goes through the alphabet with you at school and talks about how to sound out the words you'll learn that, too."

He looked down at the book in her lap as if studying it and seeing it in a new light. "I can really have adventures?"

She nodded. "Luke, you would be amazed how many adventures you can go on if you pick the right book." She opened the one in her lap. "Let's start at page one. You go as slow as you need the first time."

Across the room Jared caught Caroline staring at the two of them curled on the couch. He tugged softly on one of her braids.

"She really is a good person, Caroline." That earned him a look that was undecided and slightly embarrassed. "All she wants is a chance."

She looked down at the book in front of her. "I want things the way they were." When she looked up at him, her expression and the tears in her eyes broke his heart all over again. "I miss Mummy and Daddy."

Jared reached out and pulled her close as she buried her face in his shirt. She had been so brave, hiding her feelings most of the time, trying to take care of him and the boys.

But sometimes, out of the blue, it would get to her.

"I miss them, too, sweetheart. That's part of love." He stroked her head softly. "Your mum would be happy that Annie is here. They were very good friends."

When she didn't reply, he searched for the words he hoped would help her understand and bring her a little closer to accepting the situation that had brought Annie into their lives.

"The one thing your mother wanted was for you and Luke and Toby to grow up together."

She sniffled slightly and pulled away to look up at him, keeping her voice low. "I was afraid when that lady came to talk to you about us."

"I was afraid, too."

She looked surprised. "But you're a grown-up."

"Grown-ups get scared, too."

"You're not scared now that Annie is here, are you?"

"No, I'm not. The lady who came from the city will be happy I'm married and you and the boys will have someone to do all the things Mummy can't do for you."

Caroline closed her books and packed away her pens, setting them all together neatly on the table before looking up at him again.

"I'm scared that one day I won't be able to remember Mummy and Daddy."

In that one sentence Caroline had opened up to him more than in the months since her parents' death. "You have photos and any one of them will bring back a memory."

"I do that sometimes with the photographs by my bed," she confessed.

"You won't ever forget them, Caroline, I promise. You'll remember what they taught you and how it felt when they hugged you. You'll take them both with you wherever you go because they will always be in your heart."

She nodded, wiping her eyes with the back of her hand. "I think I'll go to bed."

She picked up her books, saying good-night to Annie and the boys as she went by.

Annie closed the book and handed it to Luke. "You did very well tonight. We'll do more tomorrow. You can watch TV with Toby until bedtime."

He didn't need to be told twice and scrambled down to sit with his brother. She stood, walking over to Jared, trying hard not to remember the look in his eyes and the husky tone of his voice earlier.

"Is she okay?"

He nodded. "She'll be fine."

"Would you like some hot chocolate before I head off to your parents' house?"

"Sounds great."

"I'll make some and then I'll put the boys to bed." She stifled a yawn. "I used to have trouble sleeping but now living here, by the time I lay down at night my body is so ready to sleep."

"No second thoughts about going through with the marriage?" He knew already what her answer would be…he just needed to hear it. "Country life is not for everyone. It's tougher than it looks."

Annie smiled. "So am I. I'm in this for the long

haul," she said. "When I fall asleep now I'm not lonely."

Jared didn't ever want her to feel alone again.

She lay in bed later and gazed out the window at the moon, so big and white and high in the sky. As so often happened, her thoughts turned to the children.

Anybody seeing the three of them together would think they were blood-related siblings from the womb. That was how close they had grown, how strong their bond was.

She wanted to nurture that bond, to help them grow into confident, happy teenagers and then adults. Maybe someday they would come home from university, or perhaps once they married they would bring their children back to visit.

Would Jared, even then, still be content with the decision he had made to ask her to marry him? Or would he look back and decide he had given up far too much?

As she drifted off to sleep, Annie prayed for guidance. She would need it over the next few months as she found her feet in this new life she had.

Maggie Stewart was in her late sixties and looked twenty years younger. Her clothing store housed a treasure chest of fashions from yesteryear, all lovingly preserved and cared for.

The morning they arrived she greeted Eve like an old friend. Maggie took a good look at Annie. Suddenly she felt underdressed in jeans and a light blouse, with sneakers on her feet. She had gotten so used to dressing casually since coming to live here.

"Red hair and green eyes. What a killer combination. No wonder Jared was bowled over!"

Annie opened her mouth to put the woman straight and then stopped. Naturally people were going to assume that she and Jared were getting married because they had fallen in love.

Eve came to her rescue. "He cares for Annie very much. Now, about those dresses in the back…"

Maggie beckoned them through the crowded little store as they stepped over boxes waiting to be unpacked.

"With your figure you can wear just about any style. I think something with a fitted bodice would suit you, but I have quite a few vintage dresses back here for you to choose from."

When Maggie opened the large walk-in closet, Annie took a breath at the beautiful old-fashioned wedding gowns that hung there.

She reached out, almost afraid to touch the lace-and-silk creations.

"Take out any you like and try them on. I'll close up the partition here and you'll have complete privacy." With that, Maggie left them alone.

Annie looked at her soon-to-be mother-in-law. "They are all so beautiful, how do I choose?"

Eve touched the younger woman's cheek in a maternal gesture. "My mother told me when I found the dress I was meant to wear on my wedding day I'd know it, I'd feel it the moment I put it on."

"And did you?"

"Of course. Didn't you know mothers are very wise?"

"Some mothers."

Chapter Six

"Oh, Annie, I am so sorry. I didn't mean to bring up a painful subject."

"You didn't. I...I've just missed having a mother and even when I had Sylvia in my life she was miserable and so unhappy."

"That isn't your fault and today I don't want you thinking about anything except finding your dress."

They pulled out dress after dress, each one lovelier than the last, each one with stitches and delicate embroidery that could never be duplicated in the modern era.

It took her almost an hour, but just as she was about to give up Annie reached into the back of the closet and pulled out the most beautiful dress she had ever seen.

She had found the one.

Eve's excitement was infectious. "Try it on."

With her help Annie stepped into the dress. It took a few minutes as Eve fussed here and there, buttoning the back, straightening and fixing as she went.

Then she stood back, a look on her face that Annie knew she would remember as long as she lived. A mother's pride. Then she saw the tears in her eyes.

Was she remembering her own daughter's wedding? Annie hadn't even thought that this might be difficult for her. "I'm sorry if this makes you sad."

Eve brushed away the tears. "When Sara got married, I was so proud. And now I get to help you and enjoy this feeling all over again. Thank you."

Eve guided her to the full-length mirror on the far wall. "What do you think?"

"Oh, my…" The rest of her sentence would remain unspoken. Annie looked at the woman staring back from the mirror and took in every lovely inch of the floor-length gown.

The cream color complemented her complexion better than she could have hoped. The neckline was rounded with a lace yoke. The slightly padded shoulders fit her perfectly. The sleeves were long, fitted and ended in a point over the top of each hand. The bodice was fitted and extended to the waistline. Around her legs, the slightly gathered skirt hung softly, from the waistline, its fullness not overly puffy but very feminine.

"This is it." She was amazed at the image that stared back at her. "This is the one."

"It looks beautiful on you," Eve replied. "Have you decided what to do with your hair?"

Annie felt so at ease with this woman that she told her the truth. "Jared asked if I would wear it down."

Eve looked stunned. "My son said that?"

Annie nodded. "Just last night."

"I'm so glad you came into our lives." She stood back and chuckled. "Mick always had a thing for my long hair, too. I think he almost cried the day I cut it off."

Annie looked in the mirror again. "I wonder how much this is?"

Eve found the sales ticket pinned to the dress. When she named the price, Annie felt guilty.

"That is not a lot of money for a wedding gown." She had interpreted Annie's silence correctly.

"It just seems a little extravagant."

"Extravagant? This is your wedding, child."

Annie knew in her heart she was going to buy the gown. "It's like something out of a fairy tale," she said. "I feel like a princess."

Eve chuckled. "I'm glad. That is the way every bride should feel when she steps into her dress. Now let's find Maggie and let her see what a perfect fit we found."

Maggie concurred. "The beading on that is very minimal but excellent workmanship."

"I'll take it."

Maggie stood with hands on hips and surveyed her. "It looks like you were born to wear that gown."

Eve helped her out of the gown and together they put it back on the hanger and covered it with the garment bag Maggie handed them.

Handling it as carefully as the precious contents demanded Annie laid the garment bag on the back seat of the vehicle. "I think we deserve lunch."

Almost on cue, Annie's stomach growled and they both laughed. "I guess that was a 'yes.'"

The day was enjoyable. They found a pair of shoes that would not only complement the dress but would also be comfortable. Against Annie's protests, Eve took her to a modern woman's boutique and made a gift of the loveliest nightgown she had ever seen.

"I know this marriage is a little unconventional, but I want you to feel like a bride on your wedding day. I hope you don't mind."

"Mind? You've taken me under your wing and brought me into your family. You have always made me feel like I had a place to belong."

"You do belong with us, dear. I only hope that once you're married, Jared begins to see what a treasure God has given to him in you."

"I'm no treas—"

"Yes, you are. You're going to change his life, Annie Dawson, and Mick and I couldn't be happier."

Jared had already changed hers. "Thank you for the nightgown. Even if nobody else sees it I'll feel very special."

Annie picked up Toby, and then it was time to get the children up from school. She made it with fifteen minutes to spare.

She had just turned off the engine when a tapping at her window had her looking. Susie smiled back and Annie put her window down.

"Jared told Danny the good news this morning when he saw him at the feed store. Congratulations."

"Thank you."

"You don't know how many times we speculated as to why Jared didn't date any one of the few dozen women who've been chasing him in town. Little did we guess that you were waiting in the wings to steal his heart."

"He's a very special man. When he asked me it was an easy answer."

Susie smiled. "I'll bet it was. When is the big day?"

"We're seeing Reverend Kane after church this weekend to see when he can schedule us in."

"If you need help with anything, you just pick up the phone, okay?"

Annie was touched by the thoughtfulness of the offer. She could tell by the tone in her voice that Susie had made it in the genuine spirit of friendship.

She had always been a bright spot Annie could recall from her school days. Many times she had even shared her lunch with Annie, some days bringing extra so there would be enough.

"I would like to invite you and Danny to the wedding."

Susie brightened like a lightbulb. "We'd love to come. I'll find a sitter for the children."

"Oh, children are welcome…if you want to bring them, that is. It's entirely up to you."

Susie thought about it for a moment. "I didn't know…these days some people just don't want children at a wedding."

"Children make a wedding special. It will give the boys and Caroline someone to play with afterward."

"You can be sure my boys are well behaved. And thanks again for the invite."

"I'll let you know the time and date."

Annie had been concentrating on the wedding for another reason. She didn't want to think about the ramifications if Jared were ever to find out about Toby—that she was the one who had given him up.

Only one other person knew the truth and Annie knew in her heart that Lewis would never breathe a word of it, not even to the man who was his best friend.

It didn't feel good keeping the secret, especially knowing how Jared felt about the subject. Guilt pricked at her conscience all the time and it was getting harder and harder to quell the turmoil inside her.

She had tried to convince herself what she was doing wasn't wrong. But even in keeping the truth from Jared, it was good as lying to him outright.

There was a chance that if she told him the truth Jared might be able to eventually see it reasonably, from her view. But she knew he wouldn't, knew in her heart, remembering the look on his face on that first day when she had broached the subject.

He would not even want her in his life and she was not about to sacrifice the happiness of the children because of a decision she made long before she even met Jared again.

She would try to live with the guilt as best she could.

That Sunday after church, Eve and Mick took the children down the street for milkshakes while Jared and Annie followed Reverend Kane into his office at the back of the building.

As they sat there with the minister, she smoothed her dress nervously until Jared took her hand calmly in his and gave her a reassuring smile that curled her toes.

"We'd like to be married as soon as possible," said Jared.

Reverend Kane looked a little worried. "Not to pry, but is anything wrong?"

Annie knew exactly what he was trying to ask in the most tactful way possible, but she blushed, anyway. "Nothing's wrong. We just want it to be soon, so the children can settle down and have some normalcy in their lives again."

The older man seemed pleased with their response "How about two weeks from today?"

Jared looked at her for confirmation. "It sounds wonderful. I invited Susie and Danny Peters. I hope you don't mind."

When Jared smiled, her whole world tilted, but not in a scary way. "Of course not."

"And your mother? She won't be attending?" The minister's enquiry was a quiet one.

"I wouldn't know where to find her."

"She was always so full of anger. I remember going out to the house many times but she would never let me in, wouldn't talk to me."

"I remember. You would bring food for us."

"And she would make me leave the boxes on the porch."

Annie felt ashamed at the way her mother had treated the man of God. "She was that way with everyone, Reverend, not just you."

He fell silent for endless moments and then he spoke. "I'm glad you found your way back to Guthrie, to our community." He looked at Jared. "You are very lucky to be getting this young lady."

"I know it. The children are lucky, too."

"You're doing a wonderful job with those kids. It's an inspiration—just what family is all about."

Annie listened as the minister went over the normal things he spoke to young couples about as they approached marriage.

His tone was businesslike but friendly, too. He spoke about the sanctity of marriage, the commitment, the love, understanding and patience that was needed. Then he talked about respect, for themselves and for each other.

"Are you okay?" They made their way lazily up the main street an hour later as they went to join his parents and the children.

"I'm fine. It's just all seeming so real now. I mean setting an actual date, having the dress…"

"Overwhelming?" He tucked her arm over his in a gallant gesture as they walked.

"A month ago I was waiting tables and going home to an empty apartment every night."

"Now you're taking on the role of wife, mother and homemaker."

Annie thought about each of those titles and what

they meant to her, what she could bring to them. "And I've never been happier. I guess things have just happened so fast."

"I'm sorry about that." He paused outside the café. "The lady from family services boxed me into a corner, or I might have put myself there telling her I was planning to get married in the future. Either way, this is the right thing to do," he said confidently. "The sooner we get this done, the sooner we can settle down with the kids to a normal life. The Lord knows they need stability."

Annie looked up at him, waiting until he met her eyes with his own. "They have you, Jared. They've had your mum and dad. Losing their parents was traumatic but together you have all given them the security they needed."

He touched her shoulder in a friendly gesture and as he did so, he ran his fingers through hair that fell down her back. "Let's go in."

Breathless at the look in his eyes, captured by the accelerated beating of her heart all she could do was nod when he opened the door for her.

Lewis arrived on Thursday afternoon, two days before the wedding. "Well, look at you!"

Annie was putting a batch of scones in the oven when she heard his voice. She turned around with a smile. "I didn't think you'd be here for another hour or two."

He walked across the room and hugged her, then set

her away from him and looked her up and down. "Rosy, flour-smudged cheeks, bright eyes. Country living…ah, I remember it well."

Jared came in the door a moment later carrying his friend's overnight bag. "Hey, find your own woman."

Something about being called Jared's woman made Annie want to tremble. Heaven forbid she should do something so silly as giggle like a schoolgirl.

"Unc Loos."

They all laughed at Toby's excited greeting from where he sat at the end of the table, playing with his own handful of dough Annie had given him.

"He'll get the hang of my name someday when he realizes there are more than five letters in the alphabet." Lewis kissed the top of the boy's head.

Annie wiped the flour from her hands and took off her apron. "Can I get you some coffee?"

"Sounds good." He pulled out a chair next to Toby.

Jared grabbed his hat off the wall hook. "I'll be back in about half an hour. I've got to pick the kids up from school."

"I can go get them if you'd rather visit with Lewis."

"Just protect my scones." Jared smiled and gave her a wink, something he'd been doing a lot lately, at odd times when she wasn't expecting it. "I have to stop off at the tractor store and see if that part I ordered came in."

"That means I get first dibs on the scones I hear calling my name." Lewis grinned. "I might leave you one or two."

Annie put a mug of coffee in front of him. "You could eat them all, I'd just make Jared another batch."

Lewis looked from Annie to Jared, his expression pleased as punch. "You're not even married and already you're spoiling him rotten."

Jared chuckled. "Do you need me to get you anything in town, Annie?"

"I have everything I need."

"I'll be back soon."

The adults sat in silence listening as the sound of Jared's truck faded in the distance. Toby spoke to himself in a language only he understood as he played.

"You look like you were made for this kitchen."

Annie let go a breath of relief. "I love it here, Lewis. Thank you so much for making it possible."

"You don't have to thank me." He looked at Toby. "I can see you in him."

She, too, looked at her son sitting at the end of the table. He glanced back at her, his smile big and cheerful, the way little boys should smile…carefree and innocent.

"I see it, too. The funny thing is when I see him with Jared and his parents, or with Caroline and Luke, I realize *they* are his family. I may have brought him into the world but Sara and James gave him a life."

The ball of dough threatened to roll off the table and Lewis caught it, giving it back to him. "And you don't think there's any way Jared would ever accept the fact that—"

"Never. I wish there were some way he could see why I did it, because the guilt is hard to live with."

"I just thought…well, you two seemed pretty cozy just now and he's definitely starting to get territorial about you." At her disbelieving look, he smiled.

"Annie, he may think this marriage is going to be a union of two people sharing nothing more than a love for these kids, but you are going to turn his world up-side down."

"I'm not trying to do that. We have an agreement, an arrangement of what this marriage will be about."

"All you have to do is be you and he won't be able to help but fall in love with you."

Annie was stunned into silence. Jared, fall in love with her? It could never happen…could it?

"You're wrong."

"Am I?" He shrugged. "We'll see."

After that he expertly changed the subject, catching her up on the latest humorous happenings at his law firm. When the scones were done Annie put them on the table with cream and jam.

No sooner had she set plates out in the middle of the table than Jared and the children came through the door.

"Uncle Lewis!"

Caroline ran over, hugging him, her school bag forgotten on the floor. Jared picked it up and put in on a corner chair.

Annie noticed Luke moved slowly through the door-way behind his uncle. "Sweetie, are you okay?" She felt his forehead.

"I feel yucky."

Jared patted his shoulder. "I'll get him some juice."

Luke settled into a chair, managing a smile for Lewis. Caroline hugged him again and kissed his cheek. "Are you staying?"

"Until Sunday."

Luke took the glass his uncle held out to him. "I want to show you the rabbits and the guinea pig when I feel better."

Caroline gained his attention again. "And then you can jump on the trampoline with me."

"Hold it a minute. I'm gifted, it's true, but even I can't do everything at once."

Jared laughed as he poured himself a cup of coffee.

"Gifted? Is that what they're calling it these days?"

Lewis shot him a look over Caroline's head. "Jealousy is a curse, my friend."

Annie served up afternoon tea as the good-natured bantering went back and forth. She kept a careful eye on Luke, who actually seemed to brighten up a little.

After dinner, Annie packed the dishwasher, smiling at the sound of laughter coming from the living room. When Jared came into the kitchen, she looked up.

"What on earth is he doing in there?"

Jared stood there, hands in his jean pockets, his shirt-sleeves rolled up to reveal strong forearms.

"He's rolling around on the floor pretending to be a giant alien and they have to get past him to reach the toy box."

"He's a good man."

Jared placed his hands on her shoulders and turned her to look at him. Annie expected the jolt that she got by meeting his eyes.

"He brought you back into my life. And you brought the sunshine with you. You're a one of a kind."

A one of a kind who was lying to him, she thought, swallowing the sick feeling in her throat. "How is Luke?"

"He fell asleep watching television so I took him up and put him to bed. I'll go check on him."

When she was alone, Annie, closed her eyes. "I can't fall in love with him."

Her purpose here was not to fall in love with a man who would never love her. Annie wasn't that fond of heartache.

The sun shone brightly on the morning of the wedding. Eve was determined that the bride and groom would not see each other before the ceremony.

She had spent yesterday afternoon getting food prepared and stored in the extra refrigerator Sara had kept in the laundry room. She had spent last night here with Annie.

Watching Jared pack up the boys to take them to spend the night with his father and Lewis had been wrenching. They hadn't planned on Caroline going along, but she was adamant.

So they had compromised. She could go with her brothers and uncle to stay the night with her grandfather, but in the morning she would come back here to get ready.

Early this morning, when it was still dark, Annie had prowled the house, actually feeling Jared's absence, missing the children even though they were only a mile away.

Luke had called her on the phone so she could say good-night to him and even Jared admitted that when Luke had handed him the phone, he couldn't wait until they were all living permanently under one roof.

Now she lay here in the spare bedroom Jared had said would be hers once they were married. Today she would say the words and make the promises the reverend asked of her.

Those vows would make her and Jared partners— friends uniting for a worthy cause.

"Annie?"

"Come in." The door opened and her soon to be mother-in-law came in balancing a breakfast tray in one hand.

"I'm spoiling you today." Annie sat up in the bed. It looked like a feast fit for a queen with an omelette, toast and a cup of tea.

"Thank you so much."

"You go at your own pace today. Mick is going to bring Caroline over here and then he'll help Jared get the boys ready."

Annie wished the little girl had thawed toward her and the marriage. Caroline had accepted that the wedding would happen, but she hadn't changed her mind about Annie or her place in their lives.

"I can only hope Caroline will want to be in the wedding photographs."

Eve sat down on the edge of the bed. "Caroline is on her own time clock. You've been patient and caring toward her. You're doing fine. Caroline usually works things out, she just takes a little longer."

"And this is a big event in her life."

"Deep down, my granddaughter knows you're not trying to replace Sara, but maybe part of her is afraid that to like you is being disloyal to her mother."

"Jared had the same thoughts."

"She'll come around, I promise. I live in hope that someday I see love in Jared's eyes for you, Annie. Every woman deserves that love…and my son deserves the chance to experience it with a kind and gentle young woman like you."

Eve walked to the door. "You have about six hours before the wedding to be lazy and relax."

"I'm going to take a nice long bath and try not to think about how nervous I am."

"I can almost assure you my son is more nervous than you are."

When she was alone, Annie leaned her head back on the pillow. "Lord, You've brought me this far. Bless what Jared and I do today and know that our marriage is born of good intentions, if not love."

Jared was up before anyone else. He'd fixed breakfast for his father and the boys in his mother's kitchen. He was just finishing up the dishes when his father came in.

"How do you feel this morning, son?"

"Like I want to be back in my own house with Annie."

His father raised an eyebrow and smiled. "Really."

"Yeah, you don't know how many times I had to read the boys their bedtime story." His father's disappointment was obvious. "Apparently I don't give all the characters different voices like Annie does."

He was not about to admit to his father that after just a few weeks, he had grown so used to having Annie here that her absences at night were starting to leave a hole.

"I'm going to get Caroline over to the house."

"She hasn't been very talkative."

Mick waved away his concerns. "She'll get used to the idea of Annie. That young lady has a way of winning people over."

Jared knew exactly what his father was speaking of. "When she asked me last week if I would give her away, I…I got choked up. I'm a very lucky man."

Jared remembered how pleased Annie had been when Mick had wholeheartedly agreed to give her away. At first she'd worried about upsetting him, but Jared had known his father would do it.

Caroline came downstairs then, her overnight bag over her shoulder.

"Do I get a hug from my best girl?"

She shrugged but put her arms around Jared. "I guess after today I won't be your best girl anymore."

Jared gave her a squeeze and set her away so he could look her in the eye. "Caroline, you are so wrong. Nothing is going to change. I told you Annie and I have one concern—keeping us together as a family."

He could see in her eyes that she didn't believe him. It would be an uphill battle with her, but Jared was determined that she would come to realize the truth.

"Come on, sweetie." Mick held out his hand. "Grandma is waiting to do your hair."

Her sigh was one of resignation. At the doorway, she turned to Jared. "I can't wait for today to be over." With an unhappy expression she was gone.

Later, with the boys down for a nap, Jared had insisted they needed to get through the day, and with Caroline gone, the house was quiet.

Jared sat at the kitchen table wondering how Annie had breathed her own brand of life back into his family in just a short space of time.

Was she nervous today? he wondered. He'd lain awake last night thinking of her in the home they'd been sharing, a house that would see them through good times and bad.

Annie wasn't the kind of woman he had ever imagined himself with. After Melanie, Jared had begun to think perhaps he was incapable of making *any* woman happy. But Annie made it seem so easy now. Around her he could be himself, he felt no pressure and they were uniting for a common cause that was close to both their hearts.

He would do the best he could so that she never regretted marrying him and being a mother to the children.

Annie was the last to get ready that afternoon. Caroline hadn't said very much to her since she arrived and obviously wasn't excited about the proceedings ahead.

Eve had enough exuberance to keep Caroline smiling at least some of the time and to save Annie from reliving her earlier bout of nerves.

Annie watched as Eve did her granddaughter's hair, drying and brushing it until it hung down Caroline's back in a shiny cascade.

The dress the little girl had chosen was emerald green, a very simple style with a deep green belt at the waist and lace on the short sleeves. She was putting on her best shoes when Annie complimented her on how beautiful she looked. Her reply was a murmured "thank you."

But if Caroline's attitude was subdued, Eve's was as lively as a firecracker and a keg of energy besides. When Annie opened the bedroom door to her a little later, Eve's exclamation made Annie smile.

"Oh my!"

Annie smoothed her hand over the delicate fabric that clung to her. "I think we picked the right dress."

Eve came into the room. "*You* picked the right dress."

"I feel funny inside, not quite nerves, and not quite butterflies."

Eve reached for Annie's veil, which was hanging near the mirror. "Don't even try to explain the feeling, Annie. I've been there and trust me, there are no words. Even now, more than thirty years later, I still couldn't describe it if someone asked me to."

Annie stood still as Eve set the veil in place. She had worked hard on her hair to get it just right. She was leaving it long today as Jared had asked.

Eve turned her toward the mirror when she was done. Secured in her hair by a seemingly invisible clip, the semicircle of small daisies and tiny rosebuds that Eve had worked on last night was the most beautiful thing she had seen.

Edged in fine lace, the veil ended just past her hips. Annie realized she had her wish. She looked very old-world Victorian.

In the mirror, she saw Caroline come to the doorway. "What do you think, sweetie? Isn't Annie beautiful?"

"You look very pretty." The words were nice but there was no warmth in her voice. Still, Annie felt hopeful.

She slipped into the white pumps she'd bought and picked up the lovely bouquet Eve had made.

A car came up the driveway. "The boys are here, both big and small." Eve let the curtain fall back into place. "And the Peterses rolled in right behind them."

Caroline was gone in an instant.

"Does Jared look nervous?"

"Jared never looks anything but totally in control," Eve said. "You have to look into his eyes to see his emotions. He can't hide it there."

Eve looked thoughtful for a moment. "The buffet is ready, the chairs are out in the garden." She cinched her bathrobe tighter around her. "I'm going to finish getting dressed. When everyone is ready and Reverend Kane arrives, I'll send Mick up for you."

Annie took a deep breath. "I'll be here."

Eve gave her one last hug. "Today is your day, Annie,

enjoy it. As far as I'm concerned, you are the best thing that has happened to my son in a long time."

Annie paced as time ticked by. She adjusted her veil and straightened her hose, nervous tension making her fuss.

When Mick knocked on the door half an hour later, Annie fought butterflies in her stomach that seemed as big as jumbo jets. He smiled the minute he saw her. How distinguished he looked in his suit and navy blue tie.

"I'm ready."

He tucked her hand in the crook of his arm. "I couldn't be more proud of you if you were my own daughter. Shall we go and get you married to my son?"

"There's nothing else I would rather do today."

Mick wore the smile all the way out of the room and was still beaming when they walked out into the backyard and into the garden that Sara and James had lovingly landscaped and planted.

Sara's beloved sunflowers made a beautiful backdrop to the day. They were the first things she saw as she walked out into the soft sunlight.

When she saw Jared, her heart sung as if a choir had burst to life inside her.

Chapter Seven

He was dressed in a black suit, white shirt and a tie of sapphire blue. From head to toe, Annie couldn't help but be impressed with the man charged with keeping her forever. When her gaze reached his face, the smile he wore hit her like a sucker punch and she fought to breathe. It was a smile of approval, as he took in her entire appearance. It was a smile of intent, a smile that seemed to tell her he was ready—he was prepared and this was what he wanted.

Annie felt sad for those women who never had a man look at them like Jared was looking at her now.

As she walked with Mick down to where Jared stood with Reverend Kane, Annie might not have managed to get her feet to move.

It became easier, however, when she spied two excited little boys standing beside Jared. In their very best church clothes, they looked like miniatures of their uncle. A butterfly distracted Toby momentarily and he was intent on catching it. Luke fiddled and fussed with the tie that he wasn't used to wearing.

Lewis stood on the other side of Jared, in his tailored suit. He smiled like a choirboy, full of mischief. He winked as she smiled back.

Annie gave a small wave to Susie and Danny, their boys seated quietly in chairs beside them. Eve and Caroline stood close to the arbor that had been constructed especially for the day.

Caroline stared at her, no expression on her face, though once she did cast a glance at her uncle to gauge his reaction to the woman walking toward them. What did she see in her uncle's expression that put the thread of sadness in her eyes?

Then there was no more thinking, or worrying. Mick brought her to a stop alongside Jared. Finally close enough to touch him, she looked up into his face.

"Your hair looks perfect," he said softly. "You look amazing."

Annie couldn't help but feel feminine pride.

"Ready?"

Annie had never felt so sure of anything in her life. "Absolutely."

Reverend Kane welcomed everyone, opened his Bible and began the ceremony. Eventually he turned to Mick.

"Who gives this woman to be joined in marriage to this man?"

Mick cleared his throat. "I do." He then shook Jared's hand before holding Annie's hand out to him.

Jared took it without hesitation, wrapping his long, strong fingers around her petite hand as if she were a lifeline he was never going to let go of.

Annie concentrated on the words that would bind her to Jared for the rest of her life. Those same words came alive as Jared repeated them in his deep, soothing voice.

The words "I do" came so naturally to her when she was asked the most important question. There was no hesitation in Jared's voice when he answered the same.

The rings they exchanged were simple gold bands that they had chosen just a few days ago. Jared had wanted to get her something with a stone in it, but she had assured him a plain gold band would mean more to her.

And then it was over. "Congratulations." Reverend Kane closed his Bible. "Jared, you may kiss your bride."

Annie froze, her fingers tightening on his. She looked up at Jared as he leaned his face close to hers. When he was close enough she whispered, "Jared, we don't have to."

"Yes, we do." His assertion was soft but firm. His hands framed her face. "You deserve that on your wedding day."

She closed her eyes. If he was doing this because he felt he had to, she didn't want to see it.

When he kissed her it was a brush of his lips on hers, not in any way meant to be romantic or intimate, but it left Jared reeling.

He had made certain to keep the kiss as generic as he possibly could and yet his hands trembled now as he pulled back and looked at her lovely face.

Her eyes opened slowly and her lips parted in a sigh. Her softly uttered "Wow" had him smiling. He took a deep breath and looked at the minister.

"I guess that makes us legal?"

"I just need some signatures and we're all done." They followed the minister to the small table that held the marriage certificate and a pen. Jared never once let go of her hand.

"Are you okay?"

Annie couldn't tell him the truth—that she was still shaking inside from the most amazing kiss she'd ever been given.

She couldn't tell him that she wouldn't mind kissing him again…many times and that even though he had meant it to be a fleeting brush of lips, it had seared her heart.

Instead, she managed what she hoped was a confident smile and nodded. "Of course."

"You did great."

She chuckled. "So did you."

"Yeah, not as scary as I always assumed it would be."

"Now we have the easy part—eating and socializing."

He put his arm around her waist. "Fortunately I do both very well."

And that cheerful voice he used set the tone for the rest of the day. The weather cooperated, the sun slipped in and out of the clouds and the breeze kept up a slight, but cooling zephyr.

Photographs were taken, it seemed, from every

angle. Annie and Jared together, without the children, then with the children, then with each child individually. His parents posed with them, as did Reverend Kane, Lewis and the Peters' family.

Jared sat beside her at the long picnic table to eat, the conversation coming easily as the assembled group recalled a lot of funny stories from the past. Annie felt so at ease. They didn't talk about tough times, or times when each of them had been through their own trials. But they did talk about people remembered, those who were no longer with them.

The children played nearby, Caroline holding the skirt of her dress down when she jumped on the trampoline. Annie didn't even want to imagine how dirty the boys would be getting playing with their trucks in the sandpit.

Luke had complained earlier that his tummy was hurting him again. He looked a little pale but he wasn't running a fever and he managed to eat a little lunch.

They were a family. Now the hard work began. Learning to live together, teaching each other, supporting and defending each other. They were a family in name, now they would work to be a family of the heart, a family of the soul.

As early afternoon eased its way into evening, gifts were presented. Lewis gave them a vacation package to the city's most popular theme park, something they could enjoy as a family.

The Peterses gave them a beautiful leather-bound photo album. "We thought it would be big enough to hold your memories of today," Susie said.

Annie smiled and hugged the woman. The album would hold photographs, the tangible memories of this day, but her heart held memories, too, and those would stay with her. She would call them to mind many times in the coming years and relive this day her life had changed forever.

Eve and Mick gave them frames, both hanging and standing, and a gift certificate to the most popular restaurant in town.

The Peterses left as the sun kissed the horizon, the very-pregnant Susie showing her exhaustion. Jared and his father began dismantling the long table while Lewis stacked chairs.

Jackets and ties had long since been discarded, sleeves rolled up as they worked.

Annie had changed out of her dress, and now wore a cotton sundress of the palest blue, with casual white sandals. Once the veil had come off she'd braided her hair to keep it out of her way.

Finally the work was done inside. Eve looked around for more to do, but Annie convinced her that she could handle everything from here on out.

"I'm going to get my husband and take him home." She picked up her handbag. "We'll have a quiet snack and put some Glenn Miller on the stereo."

Annie hoped that years from now, even though theirs wasn't a love match, she and Jared might spend an evening like the one Eve just described.

Later that evening, with Lewis already in bed, Jared and Annie took a long time with the children, getting them settled and listening to the excitement of the day they'd had.

"How do you feel, mate?" Jared asked Luke as he pulled the covers up over him.

Luke snuggled into his pillow. "My tummy still hurts a bit."

Annie felt his forehead with her hand. "You don't feel warm. Would you like a glass of water?"

Luke shook his head and sighed. They kissed him good-night as his eyes drifted closed.

Toby was already asleep as they turned out the light and pulled the door up. "Caroline's light is off," said Jared. "I guess she's asleep already."

Annie stifled a yawn. "It has been a long day."

"Yes, it has. Do you think Luke is okay?"

Annie was also worried that the child could be coming down with something. "We'll watch him closely. I know he's been feeling tired but he seemed okay playing today."

Jared smiled. "Maybe I'm overreacting."

Annie put a hand on his arm. "It's not a crime, it's natural."

Natural, he thought. It was also natural for a man to take his beautiful new bride to bed on their wedding night. Right now, standing here looking at her, it seemed like the most natural thing in the world to do.

But he didn't. Instead he remembered how much of his heart doing something like that would cost him. He'd promised her a platonic marriage.

She had agreed to that, perhaps because she wanted

to be a mother to the children so badly, perhaps because of the person she had hinted about in her past.

"I guess this is good night."

Annie nodded. "What are we going to do after church tomorrow?"

"Let's take it as it comes, see what we feel like."

Annie smiled as she opened her bedroom door. "Sounds fine."

"Good night, Annie," he said. "And thank you for saying yes."

The emotion of the day welled inside her and she blinked back moisture in her eyes. "Thank you for asking me," she said. "Good night, Jared."

She was about to close her door when he called her name. He stood there looking so handsome.

"Sleep tight."

Something told her they were not the words he'd been planning to say. He disappeared down the hall and she heard his bedroom door close.

She closed her door and turned down her bed, her mind a whirl of images, thoughts and questions. Tomorrow, she thought, the wedding would be in the past and they could get on with the business of being a family.

Tomorrow was the first day of the rest of her new life. And, smiling, she sent a prayer of thanks heavenward and fell asleep with a heart full of hope.

"Annie, wake up."

Never a heavy sleeper, Annie looked at the alarm

clock. It was still three hours until dawn. She sat up in bed and looked at Jared.

"What is it?"

"I need to take Luke to the hospital," he said, buttoning the shirt he had just thrown on. He left it hanging outside his jeans. "He's been vomiting and has a fever. He's also complaining of a pain in his side."

Annie was out of the bed with his first words, collecting her clothes from the chair nearby. "Appendicitis?"

"I think it is, but he needs to see a doctor. I already called ahead. They're expecting us at the hospital."

"I'm coming with you."

Relief showed in his worried eyes. "I thought you'd feel that way. Caroline and Toby are still asleep. Lewis is making coffee so he'll be up if they wake."

He left the room to see to Luke, and Annie wasted no time getting dressed. She dragged on jeans and her tennis shoes. She pulled a sweatshirt over her head and quickly brushed her hair back into a ponytail.

She was waiting for him by the front door, a worried Lewis beside her as Jared came down the stairs with Luke in his arms, a quilt wrapped around him.

The little boy moaned and held a small bowl. "Annie." His voice was soft, fear mixing with the tears in his eyes. "It hurts."

"I know it does." She smoothed her hand over his forehead, noting the heat and the moisture. "I'm here, sweetie."

Annie hopped up into the vehicle, holding out her arms as Jared placed Luke in her comforting embrace.

"Call me when you know anything," Lewis said.

They made the trip into town in what had to be record time. Annie held Luke securely all the way, whispering to him that everything would be okay, kissing his head and trying to soothe him in any way she could.

When they pulled up at the entrance to the small country hospital, a nurse met them at the door. "The doctor was here for another emergency." Jared came around the car. "He waited for you."

"Thank God."

He took Luke from Annie and followed the nurse.

Hospitals, she decided, were the same everywhere—quiet, almost solemn and always smelling impossibly sterile and clean.

The doctor couldn't have been much older than Jared. He examined Luke with skill and care, asking the boy questions and nodding noncommittally when he answered.

Jared held Annie's hand as if it were a lifeline.

"We'll get him admitted. His appendix needs to come out now." The urgency in his voice was not lost on either of them.

"Uncle Jared? Am I…going home?" Luke whimpered softly through another bout of pain.

Jared leaned down and brushed a kiss on the boy's forehead. "The doctor needs to take out your appendix, mate."

He started to cry. "Then will you take me home?"

"Just as soon as the doctor says we can."

After that it was a hive of activity. The doctor suggested it might be better if one of them stayed with Luke while they administered the anesthetic.

Annie offered and Jared nodded, fishing in his pocket for change. "I'll go call Mum. Then I'll call Lewis and tell him we'll be here for a while. I want to be here when Luke wakes up so he's not alone."

"We'll both be here."

Jared kissed his nephew and told him he'd see him in just a while. Luke was doing his very best to be brave.

Jared barely made it out of the room before his eyes welled up with tears. Just the thought of Luke being in pain, the thought of him undergoing surgery, was almost unbearable.

Yet as he dialed his mother's number he gave a silent prayer of thanks that it was something treatable, that in a few days Luke would be back home, with only a scar on his side to show for this trauma.

The call to his mother didn't last long, and he was hanging up as Annie found him in the hallway.

"Mum offered to come down and wait with us. I told her we'd keep her informed."

Annie settled on a bench along the wall. "There isn't much anyone can do, but I can understand why she'd want to be here."

Jared sat down beside her, his elbows resting on his knees as he leaned forward and hung his head. "I should have seen yesterday that something was wrong."

"He said he was feeling yucky. That could have been

anything. We did the best we could, we watched him all evening."

Jared didn't care. "He barely made it into my room before he collapsed on the floor."

"This is not your fault, Jared, and don't you dare take it on your shoulders. You don't need to be blaming yourself for something nobody could have seen coming."

He looked at her, as if seeing a new, determined side of her.

"I won't let you do this to yourself. Luke is going to need us to be cheerful and encouraging when he wakes up."

"You're right. I'm going to find some coffee in this place. Would you like juice or water if they don't have tea?"

"Anything but coffee." As he walked away she called his name and he turned. "Luke is going to be fine."

Jared didn't say a word, but walked off down the hall with a renewed sense that with Annie by his side and in their lives, things would always turn out okay.

Annie walked toward him as he came back with the drinks. "Is it Luke?"

"No. The nurse told me they have a Sunday morning service in the chapel here for patients and visitors who can't get to church."

Jared handed her a can of soda. "What if he's back in his room and wakes before it's over?"

"The nurse said she'd come and get us."

That settled it for Jared. They found the small chapel and took a seat among a handful of people—some dressed in hospital gowns and robes, some in wheelchairs, some obviously family members visiting loved ones.

Jared kneeled before God with Annie by his side on the day they should have been getting used to married life, embarking on their future.

Instead he was in this cold sterile hospital, praying that God keep another member of his family safe from harm as doctors worked on Luke. He looked up at the cross above the minister and it reminded him that the Lord's arms were outstretched to everyone.

Luke would be fine, he had to believe that. Such a merciful God would not allow them to go through another tragedy.

Jared has such a tight hold on Annie's hand that it eventually went numb, but she stayed silent, preferring to be of any support she could be to him.

Despite her earlier warning, he blamed himself. She could see it in his eyes, in the anguished expression he wore when he spoke of Luke.

Annie closed her eyes and listened to the words of the service, to the minister bless and lead prayers for the sick and those who were fighting for their lives.

Luke would be fine. Annie had to believe that. Because the thought of their family without him in it was too devastating to even contemplate.

"How do you feel, mate?"

Luke licked his lips and blinked, still drowsy but becoming more aware of his surroundings. "It hurts. Can I go home today?"

Jared patted his hand. "Not today, but in a few days." The fear in Luke's eyes cut to his soul. "One of us will always be here with you."

"Hey, am I gonna have a scar?"

Annie smiled. "I'm sure of it."

"Wow, just like a pirate."

It was at that moment Jared knew it would be okay. The doctor wanted to keep him for a few days just to monitor him, but the operation had been successful.

As the morning wore on, Luke drifted off to sleep again. Annie refilled his glass with ice chips and the pitcher with water.

Jared watched his nephew sleep. Life really was a fragile thing. As indestructible as kids usually appeared, they were the most vulnerable of all.

He was just about to tell Annie to go home and get some rest when his parents appeared in the doorway to the hospital room.

Eve's gaze went straight to Luke. "How is he?"

"Happy that he's going to have a pirate scar and already wanting to go home."

Eve leaned over and kissed her grandson's cheek. Mick pulled a vacant chair up beside the bed. "He'll be bouncing around in no time."

Annie came out of the bathroom carrying a washcloth. "Is this for Luke?" Annie nodded as Eve took it from her. "We're going to stay with him. I want you both to go home and get some sleep."

Annie and Jared protested at the same time but Eve would not hear of it. "You're both exhausted. Go home and let me do this for my grandson…for the two of you. Come back later today."

Annie could see Jared was still ready to stand his ground, but she also knew how important this was to Eve, how she needed to do this for Luke.

"Caroline is going to be wondering how he's doing," she reminded Jared. "If we go home at least we can try to put her mind at rest."

He shrugged and sighed deeply. "I can't fight the both of you."

Mick chuckled softly. "You're learning, son."

Jared couldn't even manage an answering smile. "Call when you need one of us to relieve you."

His mother hugged them both. "I brought my cross-stitch. And your father has some reading to catch up on."

She shooed them out the door and they walked in silence to the car park. The sun was just peeking over the horizon, painting the sky all colors of pink and orange.

"Would you like me to drive?"

Jared fished the keys from his pocket. "Thanks, but I'm fine."

When Annie walked in the front door to their home her first instinct was to climb those stairs and crawl right into bed.

But sitting at the bottom of the stairs was a little girl who looked more scared than Annie had ever seen her. When Jared held out his arms, Caroline ran to him.

"Is Luke dead?"

"No, Possum, didn't Uncle Lewis tell you what happened?"

She nodded against his shoulder. "But people can die from appendix attacks. Is he going to be okay?"

"Luke is going to be just fine. Grandma and Grandpa are with him now." She cast Annie a glance, then looked away.

Lewis was in the kitchen with breakfast already waiting for them when they walked in. Caroline sat down next to Jared, as if needing the security of being near him.

She seemed a little more settled and even managed to eat a little breakfast. Her first thought was to go to the hospital and see her brother. Lewis promised to take her later that morning.

Annie got Toby up and dressed, shooing Jared off to bed.

With Toby alternately following her around or chasing the cats around the yard as she pinned laundry on the line, Annie managed to get through a lot of chores and even packed some things into Luke's backpack to take to him later that evening.

When Lewis finally managed to get her off to bed, promising that he could handle a toddler without any problem, Annie climbed the stairs to her room and sank into a sleep that lasted until early that afternoon.

Jared was in the kitchen when she came downstairs. He put a cup of tea on the table as she sat down.

"How do you feel?"

"Better, thanks. Where is everyone?"

"Lewis took Caroline to the hospital. Toby's napping upstairs."

Annie stirred sugar into her tea and sipped it. "I think she'll feel a lot better about it when she sees him."

"Mum called and Luke's doing fine."

Annie's smile was one of relief. "Good."

He poured himself a mug of coffee and sat down opposite her. "It looks like we passed our first crisis as parents."

"Yes, we did."

"I was terrified," he said honestly. "I learned to cope with the loss of my sister and James because the kids needed me to be strong, but if anything were to happen to any of them…"

Annie reached over and placed her hand on his. "The kids are fine. Another day or two and Luke will be back here so full of energy you won't be able to tell anything was wrong."

He shook his head. "How were we so blessed to find you, Annie?"

"I consider myself blessed, too."

"Tell me something. This person you talked about before we were married, the person you lost…it was a man?"

Suddenly into her mind popped an image, laughing, mischievous eyes and a smile so sweet. "Chris was only nineteen when he died."

"And he was special to you?"

"Yes, he was."

"He loved you." It wasn't a question, just a statement.

"Yes."

Jared sat back in his chair. "I'm glad you knew that with him." Jared was surprised that he actually meant it.

"You deserve that kind of love."

"And now with you and the children I've found another kind of love. Family love, ties that bind the heart and the soul."

Whatever he might have said remained a mystery as Lewis and Caroline came in the door, full of news about Luke.

"He's sitting up in bed and everything!"

Lewis concurred. "He looks good for everything he's been through."

"I'll bet he was happy to see you."

Caroline's exuberance seemed to fade as she looked at her and shrugged. Annie felt hurt. She had known it would take time, but she wanted this child to at least trust her if not like her.

"I'm going to check on Toby." She heard Jared talking to Caroline as she left the room. Annie had a horrible feeling that he could talk to his niece until he was blue in the face, but it wasn't going to make any difference.

She seemed as determined now to dislike Annie as she had been when they first met. Time seemed only to be driving a wedge further between them.

Toby was awake when she checked on him. He held out his arms to her the moment he saw Annie. She walked over to him and scooped him up. She inhaled his scent, that baby smell that never quite went away. His hair so soft against her hand, his cheek so cool against her neck.

This child had saved her life, though he would never know it. His birth had proven to her that some of the most life-altering things happen when you least expect them and that love could come in so many different forms. The time she had spent here, getting to know him day by day, somehow had erased all the time she had missed, all the little milestones she hadn't shared.

The future stretched out, promising more events that she would be involved in and witness to. She would get to help shape his life and the lives of his siblings.

This was her family now and Annie was not about to give up on any of them.

That night at the hospital the whole family gathered. Luke was excited by all the visitors, but sad that Lewis was going back to the city.

"Can't you stay longer? We didn't get to do anything."

Lewis kissed his forehead. "I'll be visiting again, sport. You get better so we can do all those things we missed this time."

Luke smiled. "Okay."

Caroline sat perched on the side of his bed, asking Luke all kinds of questions.

"I told the nurses all about you, Annie."

She chuckled. "I hope some of it was good."

He looked at her with a puzzled frown. "All of it was good. I told them you married Uncle Jared and you were going to help take care of us. And I told everyone you're real pretty."

"Not as pretty as Mummy." Caroline silenced the room.

Luke glared at his sister. "She is, too. You just don't like her."

Caroline glared right back at him. "I don't have to like her. I didn't want her to come live here with us in the first place."

"Caroline!"

At her grandmother's shocked tone, she hopped off the bed and ran out of the hospital room. Jared made a move toward the door, but Annie stopped him. "Caroline and I need to have a talk."

She found the girl sitting on the front steps of the hospital. "I don't care if they all hate me. I'm not going to forget about Mummy and Daddy like Luke is."

"No one in that room hates you, Caroline. In fact, the people in there love you more than life itself."

When she didn't answer, Annie continued, "And they're going to love you for the rest of your life, no matter what you do. Your uncle was hurt. He's hurt because he did what he thought was best to keep you all together and it's made you angry and sad."

"I...I just want things back the way they were." The little girl sounded vulnerable all of a sudden.

Annie sat down on the step beside her, keeping a good distance, wanting her to know she was not about to force anything.

"We all do, Caroline."

"*You* don't."

Chapter Eight

"Because my parents died, you got to come here and marry Uncle Jared."

"You're wrong. If I could put things back the way they were, I'd do it in a heartbeat. I'd do it because I know the pain your uncle feels when he thinks about not having his sister anymore, so your grandparents could have their daughter back."

When she paused, Caroline finally looked across at her, tears in her eyes.

"I'd do it so Toby could have his mum to tuck him in at night and Luke could play soccer again with his dad. And I'd do it so you didn't feel hurt and scared, so they could see all the wonderful things you're going to do in your life."

Annie stood up after a few moments of silence and wiped her hands on the back of her jeans. "Caroline, if you don't like me that's okay, but please don't upset Luke or make him feel like he's doing something wrong by liking me. I'm glad he likes me. Before I came here I was alone, and now I have this wonderful family where I can belong."

With that she left Caroline to think about what had been said and went back inside. There was an edge of tension in the air when she went into Luke's room.

When Toby yawned and laid his head on Jared's shoulder, Annie held out her arms and the child went willingly. She looked at Jared.

"Caroline's sitting outside for a while. I'll get Lewis to drop me home on his way out of town. Toby's had a big day."

"We'll all go."

"Luke still has another hour of visiting time left. You and your parents stay and keep him company. We'll be fine."

"Annie, if Caroline said something to you outside—"

"We both said what we needed to say and we've come to an understanding. I'm leaving it up to her."

Jared ran a hand through his hair. "I'm sorry she's being like this."

"We both know why, she's scared. Let's face it, we've both been the frightened child she is." She reached up and smoothed a worry line from his forehead. "Give her time."

Eve kissed her cheek. "Go home and have a nice long bath when you put Toby down. You deserve to pamper yourself."

With Toby in her arms, she walked to the edge of

Luke's bed. She was greeted with a pair of outstretched arms and a big smile.

"I don't care what Caroline says, I love you."

Annie fought back tears at his words. She pulled back from the hug and smiled down at him. "I love you, too, Luke."

"Hey, am I supposed to call you Aunty Annie now?"

"It's up to you. Whatever you're comfortable with."

"I like just plain Annie."

"Then just plain Annie it is."

"Will you come see me tomorrow?"

"I sure will."

Jared caught up with Annie as she reached the door. "Are you sure you're all right?"

"You need to stop worrying so much. I'm fine. I'm a little tired so I may just take your mother's advice, then make myself some tea."

"We'll be home soon."

Annie wanted to hug him so badly, just to feel strong, solid arms around her. She hadn't felt that in such a long time. "I'll be there."

"And that is why it's home again."

With that he kissed Toby, the child almost asleep in her arms. Lewis came out of the room and hugged Jared.

"Take care, man."

"You, too."

Lewis looked at her. "You ready to hit the road?"

Annie nodded and followed him down the hallway. Caroline turned when they came outside and when

Lewis leaned down and hugged her, Annie heard a sniffle.

When Lewis let her go she wiped her eyes with the back of her hand and turned to go inside.

Back at the house, Lewis loaded his things into the car.

"Well, kiddo, guess this is it."

Annie hugged him, grateful once again for his friendship. "Take care of yourself. Better still, find a wild woman who'll keep you on your toes and get married."

He hugged her then set her away from him. "The best woman I know is already married." He gave her a wink as he got into the car.

"The day Jared tells you he's in love with you is the day I say 'I told you so'."

Annie smiled but didn't reply. "Have a safe trip."

She watched him until he was just a fast-moving dot on the landscape. She would never hear Jared say those words. He would never love her.

But she would be the best wife she could be. She had all the ingredients of a good life, a happy life. She had faith that Caroline would accept her in time.

After her bath, she dressed in pajamas and her long cotton robe. With her hair braided, she stepped into slippers, checked on Toby asleep in his bed and laid down for just a while in her own room to wait for Jared and Caroline.

He found her there later, curled up on top of the bed covers, her head pillowed on her hands. He'd seen the hurt in her eyes when she'd followed Caroline outside tonight. He'd seen the resolve in those same eyes when she'd come back in and taken Toby from him.

Annie was a strong woman—strong inside where it mattered. He knew in his heart she was the best thing for these kids.

But curled up here now, she looked very young.

He heard Caroline getting ready for bed, and hoped that what he'd said to her on the way home would make some impact. She was suffering; he understood that.

The death of her parents wasn't something Caroline was going to get over anytime soon—none of them were. It would take time, but that time would drag by if she didn't let anybody in, if she stayed angry with the one woman who would help her most.

They were all doing the best they knew to get through this time. He knew what it was like to lose a mother and so did Annie.

Tonight he'd been honest with Caroline about how it felt, about how he understood. He'd searched for the words, slowly hoping each one found its way to her heart to soothe her hurting.

Annie woke to a dark room, the moonlight trying to creep in through heavy curtains. Still trembling, she reached up with one hand and wiped tears from her cheeks. It had been a bad dream. She couldn't recall it even now, but it had made her feel lost, alone and abandoned. She hadn't felt like that in a long time.

She got out of bed as quietly as she could and slid

her feet into the slippers by the side of the bed. She reached for her robe and put it on, tying it at the waist.

She checked on Toby, who was sleeping soundly and snoring softly. When she opened Caroline's door, the little girl was facing the window. Annie didn't go in. She closed the door quietly.

The night air was cool when she opened the front door and went outside to sit on the veranda steps. She'd forgotten how silent the country was at night and how, away from the city lights, the night sky out here was a blanket of stars.

As she sat there, the events of the past few days caught up with her. The rush of feeling when she saw Toby again, the emotion of her wedding, the feelings for Jared she was trying to understand, then Luke getting sick.

She didn't even try to stop the tears this time. It felt therapeutic just to let it all out. She cried for Sara and James and she cried for her mother. She shed tears for the father she had never known, for Chris who had missed out on so much of life and never seen his son.

"Did I make you cry?"

Startled, Annie turned to see Caroline standing there, her eyes troubled, biting her bottom lip.

Annie wiped the tears away and sniffled. "No, sweetie, I had a bad dream."

"I have them sometimes." She sat on the step beside Annie. "I heard you come downstairs."

"I tried to be as quiet as a mouse."

"Can I ask you something?"

Annie hugged her knees and looked across at the girl. "Sure."

"Why were you alone before you came here? Didn't you have a family?"

"I have a mother but...she never really was happy being my mother. She had a lot of hurt in her life and she could never find much to be thankful for."

"What happened to your dad?"

"He died before I was born."

Her pause lasted just a few seconds. "Do you still love your mum?"

Annie thought about the question. Did she still love the woman who had shunned her at every turn and treated her like a burden, yet who had refused to let her be taken away?

"I don't understand a lot of what she went through and I can't really know why she couldn't let herself love me but yes, part of me will always love her."

Just like part of her would always hope that someday her mother would love her.

Caroline thought for a moment. "I had a family before I came to live here."

Annie didn't dare breathe. Caroline was sharing her past. There was no animosity in her tone, no hostility.

"My real dad was a policeman. I still have a picture of him up in my room. He used to make Janice laugh and he'd throw me up in the air and catch me again."

Janice was her mother, the woman who had given her away. Jared had told her that the little girl never called her anything else since coming to live here.

"He sounds like a very nice man."

Caroline smiled slightly. "He was. Then he died. Janice didn't laugh anymore. Until she met Alan." The man's name was said with a cold tone.

"He wasn't nice to you?"

"Alan had kids of his own. He didn't have to be nice to me."

"What were his children like?"

She shrugged. "They didn't like me very much."

Caroline stopped and Annie remained silent. This was a story she wanted to share. To Annie it was a gift.

"Janice married Alan and he decided he didn't want a little girl that didn't belong to him." She rested her chin on up-drawn knees. "Janice told me she had a new life now, other children. She couldn't keep me with her."

"Oh, Caroline." Annie's heart broke…for the scared child who had faced that reality.

"I was a ward of the state for almost a year."

Annie knew those were words that no nine-year-old should be familiar with, let alone understand their meaning.

"Then Mummy found out about me and brought me out here. I couldn't believe it. She already had Luke and she still wanted me. Then she brought Toby home, too."

Annie reached out and touched Caroline's shoulder. "Sara saw what we all do—a sweet girl with a good heart and a pretty smile."

Caroline smiled then, the first honest-to-goodness, real smile Annie had gotten from her in the time she'd been here. It faded slowly.

"I was afraid for a long time that they would change their mind and send me back or that I would do something to make them sad and they wouldn't want me. But even when I made mistakes they didn't ever send me back."

Annie knew Sara would have loved her more for those mistakes, and the other woman would have seen the fear and the worry and she would have worked to erase it.

"I didn't hate you, Annie, not really. When I met Alan I was nice to him because he made Janice happy. Then I saw how happy you made Uncle Jared, how much he smiled. I thought you would make me go away."

"Sweetie, that would never happen."

Caroline looked at her with uncompromising honesty. "It happened once. The person who was supposed to love me and take care of me could send me away…so why couldn't you?"

From Caroline's perspective, the threat had seemed all too real. And her reasoning was that of a child, seeing through everything to the way things were.

She took a chance and slid closer to the girl, reaching out and taking her hand, closing her fingers around it. "Why don't you let me tell you how it is?"

"Okay," came the hesitant reply.

"You are my family now, at least as far as I'm concerned. You and Luke and Toby are all in my heart and that is where you will stay."

"Forever?"

Annie smiled. "As long as forever lasts. As long as I can be here."

"What about when you and Uncle Jared have babies?"

"Caroline, I don't know that we will. But if we did, they would be additions to this family, not replacements."

"Uncle Jared likes having you here."

Annie smiled. "I like being here, with him and with you and the boys." She put her arm around Caroline and hugged her gently, pleased when she didn't pull away.

She rested her chin on the child's head. "There is something I learned awhile back. You don't have to have a baby to be a parent. There are people who have babies and just can't be parents for whatever reason. I wish you didn't have that hurt in your past, but I wouldn't change a thing about you being here. Neither would your parents or Uncle Jared. Do you know why?"

"Because they love me." It was a reply filled with certainty.

"You're a smart girl."

"That's what Uncle Jared said on the drive home." Caroline pulled away and looked up at her. "I'm always going to love Mummy and Daddy."

"I wouldn't have it any other way."

"But I would like you to be my friend."

"Sweetie, I would like that very much."

"If I have babies when I grow up, I'm going to love them so much they won't ever be scared or sad or unhappy," Caroline said with childlike simplicity.

The screen door opened and they looked around to find Jared standing there. The look on his face was one that would stay with Annie the rest of her life. She didn't know how much of the conversation he had heard, but he would be relieved that it had taken place.

When he held out his arms to Caroline, she ran to them. "No matter what happens in the future, Annie and I couldn't live without you here. We would never, ever send you away."

She nodded her understanding.

"Thank you for letting Annie in." He smoothed the hair from her face. "It wasn't so scary, was it?"

"Not really."

"I'm proud of you, Caroline."

Her smile was a bashful one, but it was there. "But I didn't do anything."

"You gave Annie a chance, you trusted me when I asked you to."

"I love you, Uncle Jared."

Jared felt a lump lodge in his throat, but he swallowed and nodded. "I love you, too, Possum. Do you feel like going back to bed?"

"I guess I'd better. I have school."

She turned toward Annie, hesitated, then leaned down to hug her. Annie put her arms around the girl and held her tight. "I'm glad we're going to be friends."

Caroline pulled away and nodded. "Me, too."

With a quick good-night she went back into the house.

"You are amazing."

Annie felt embarrassed by Jared's compliment. She stood up to face him. "I really didn't do anything to coax her into talking to me tonight."

He came toward her slowly, and when he stopped they were separated by inches. "You were patient even when she tried you. You were kind when she was hostile." His hand cupped her chin. "You were loving and caring no matter what she said to you."

"I love her."

Jared hugged her then, a spontaneous gesture, enveloping her in his embrace.

Annie clung to him, savoring the feel of his strong arms around her, the steady beat of the heart beneath his chest that sounded in her ear.

"You make me wish for things," he confessed. "You make me want what my parents share." He pulled back to look at her.

Would he still feel that way if he knew the secret she kept from him? Would that look of wonder in his eyes change to contempt if he found out she had given up her son?

Annie's hands trembled where they rested on his arms. "I won't ever hurt you, Jared. You can trust that."

The kiss he placed on her forehead was as tender as it was sweet, then he let her go with a reluctant sigh. "That's what you don't understand. I've trusted you for a long time in all the ways that matter. With the children, with their happiness, with my worries and my doubts."

Annie knew in an instant because of one untold truth, that trust could be shattered and lost to her forever.

She pulled one hand free of his and laid her palm against his cheek. "You know I'm attracted to you," she said breathlessly.

"But you have to be ready to fight the pain that holds you captive."

"I don't know if I can. I've held it like a shield around me for so long."

"You don't need it anymore."

She knew by the look in his beautiful eyes that he was fighting a war within himself, that for him this marriage was changing. When he leaned forward and placed a gentle kiss on her lips, featherlight and brief, it told her all the things he could not.

He turned and went inside. Annie stood there, her thoughts and emotions running riot through her.

The feel of his lips on her skin lingered in a determined fashion. Annie prayed right then and there, beneath the black sky blanketed with millions of bright stars, beneath a moon that was dazzling and full.

She prayed she could survive falling in love with him because it was already happening. She prayed for an end to the guilt that kept clawing at her.

She prayed that someday those scars might lose their power over him and would heal enough to set him free.

The month that followed was the closest thing to contentment Annie had known in her life. The guilt didn't abate, but it was the price she had to pay for the decision and commitment she had made.

Jared had not talked of their last kiss, but he let her

know every day in many ways that there was hope for them to go forward and explore new territory. He would hug her, touch her arm and take her hand in his, all without the indecision and hesitancy he had once felt. He was testing the waters slowly each time he reached out.

He worked hard to get the crops planted, to put in new fences and get livestock to markets. Most evenings he came in hot and sweaty, exhausted and dusty. Yet he was always smiling. He was always happy. The work seemed to invigorate him, spur him on to do even more. He would share his day with her and ask how hers was.

For her part, Annie had turned the soil in the flowerbeds and pulled weeds from what was left of the vegetable gardens.

With Toby nearby, she would spend most every afternoon out in the yard on her hands and knees reveling in the soil between her fingers, the clear smell of country.

They were slowly falling into the routine that husbands and wives fell into, the changes in their familiarity with each other and their comfort level coming very subtly.

Her friendship with Caroline had been slow to get going, the awkwardness of all that had gone before making the girl a little shy. But slowly, she was coming out of herself more and more around Annie. They did things together Annie knew she would have done with Sara.

Luke made a wonderful recovery from his operation

and now used any excuse to show off the scar he had. Annie looked forward to each and every day and was even excited, for the first time in a long while, about the approach of her birthday. It did not matter that nobody knew it was coming in two weeks. She already had the best gifts in the world, a place to belong and a family to love.

Annie's birthday did not get off to a stellar start. Her alarm clock had gone off an hour later than normal. On checking it, she found it had been changed. She dressed and went downstairs, smiling when she stepped into the kitchen.

"Surprise!"

Annie could hardly believe it. Half-a-dozen balloons were tied to the back of her chair, the sign crafted by children's hands hung on the wall. And the four people who meant the most to her in the world were standing there smiling.

"Oh my!"

The kids came forward and hugged her one by one, all wishing her happiness for the day. They led her to the table and sat her down.

Luke brought toast, Caroline filled her glass and Toby stood behind her chair, playing with the balloons and giggling.

When Jared placed breakfast in front of her and settled all the children at the table, he sat down opposite her. "Happy birthday from all of us, Annie."

"Thank you." Emotion overwhelmed her. Jared cleared his throat. "We usually reserve grace for Sunday lunch or dinnertime, but this morning I'd like to say grace."

They joined hands around the table and bowed heads.

"Lord, I thank You for all the gifts that have been brought into my life. Thank You for the children who make me want to be a better person. Thank You for the land I get to farm, the fresh air I breathe and the warm and happy home I come to each evening."

He squeezed Annie's hand as he spoke the words and she returned the gesture.

"And thank You for the woman I have in my life, for her understanding, her support and her friendship. For all these blessings I am grateful. Amen."

His last, softly spoken word was echoed around the table and when Annie looked up she found him staring at her, searching for something she could only guess at.

"It isn't every day you turn twenty-two. Make the most of it."

"They say it's downhill after twenty-one. I don't believe it, though." She looked at each of the children, then at him. "My road in life looks wonderful from where I'm sitting."

The day passed slowly and Annie savored every minute of every hour. Eve called later that morning and made her promise to come to dinner.

When they arrived that evening, Annie got the second surprise of the day. Eve, Mick and Lewis stood in the living room.

There were gifts. There were balloons and streamers. Annie did cry this time. These people who had known her as a child, and who had come to mean so much to her, had cared enough to mark this day as hers. This was the first time she could remember that her birthday had been a cause for celebration for anyone. She wiped away the tears long enough to receive hugs.

Jared watched his family embrace her. She hadn't seen the dinner his mother had prepared yet or the homemade cake. But there was no disguising the happiness in her smile, the light in her eyes and the love in the hugs she gave the people in this room.

His feelings for her were changing, slowly but surely. Every day he confronted more and more of the issues he wrestled with. And he became familiar with the idea that falling in love with Annie might make the risk of loving someone worth it.

Was this what Melanie had felt for him? he wondered. Was this why she had demanded so much of him, even as he pushed her away?

Jared confronted these feelings for Annie head-on, took them out as best he could and examined them. Some days it was all he thought about while he was working. He wanted them to be husband and wife in every way. They already had a better foundation for their relationship than some couples ever had.

He wanted these things with Annie that he'd never wanted with anyone before, but it was hard to let down the walls he had kept around himself for so long.

Loving her meant taking a risk and being prepared to trust.

* * *

Annie was spoiled that night. Dinner was wonderful, the cake beautifully decorated by Eve. Later that evening, it was time for gifts.

Lewis gave her gift certificates to various stores in town, and for such an amount of money that Annie almost felt guilty…almost. It was just so nice to think she could save them and buy things when she needed.

Eve and Mick gave her a quilt, one that had been lovingly hand-stitched. Eve admitted she'd started working on it soon after the first time Jared had brought her back from the city.

Then Caroline had presented her with a beautiful leather-bound journal. Annie hadn't kept a journal in such a long time, but now the prospect was soothing. Jared and the boys gave her a beautiful watch and a matching pair of earrings. But the gift that had taken her breath away had come from the four of them…her family.

It was a photograph, one she already had a place for on the wall at home. It had been taken on their wedding day. Jared stood tall and proud, looking so dashing! Annie looked at herself standing beside him and still had trouble believing that bride with the radiant smile was her. In front of them stood the children, amazingly all looking at the camera, all smiling, even Caroline. Annie remembered Jared had leaned down and whispered something to her just before his mother had snapped the picture.

This was their first family photograph, something

she could look at any time over the rest of her life and remember the emotions and the wonder of that day.

On their way home that night, Annie wore a glowing smile that lit Jared's heart. The dinner had been wonderful, full of laughter and chatter.

Annie sat in the front of the vehicle, her gifts wrapped securely in the folds of the quilt. "Tonight was lovely. It's the first birthday party I've ever had."

Jared schooled his expression not to register surprise. He didn't want to remind her of her past any more than she wanted to be taken back there.

"I'm glad it made you smile."

"And thank you for the photograph. All my gifts were wonderful. But that picture of us all…it just touched my heart."

"I knew it would. I hope I chose the right frame. There were so many in the store."

"It's perfect." She thought for a moment, then added. "Your family is…" The words she thought of seemed so inadequate to describe the love she felt for them.

"I know what you mean. They've left me speechless many times."

Annie knew she would never be able to explain it fully. When Eve hugged her, she felt a motherly bond with this woman that she had never found with her own.

When Mick got into a conversation with her, she liked to believe it would have been like this with her father. They had become more her parents in the last two months than she had known in her life.

It was amazing that all her life she had wanted nothing more than to get away from this town, from her mother and the house they'd lived in, away from the gossip and the stares.

But she hadn't ever forgotten the kindness of Sara and her family. Somehow, the last few years had been pointing her back here, pointing her toward home.

She had found what she had so desperately wanted when she left–a family and a place to belong.

"It was hard saying goodbye to Lewis again. I wish he could have stayed the night."

"He has some big court appearance tomorrow afternoon he needed to prepare for, but you had to know he wouldn't have missed your birthday."

At the house, Jared finally managed to settle the boys down, while Annie peeked in on Caroline. "I just came to say good night."

Caroline smiled. "Would you brush my hair? Mummy used to do it for me."

Annie felt like she'd been handed the moon and the stars. She settled on the bed behind Caroline and took the brush, beginning with soft, smooth strokes down the long blond hair.

"I hope the present I got you was okay. Mummy used to keep a journal. She had one since she was my age."

Annie remembered how worried Caroline had looked as she'd opened the gift, so afraid it wouldn't please her.

"I love it. Thank you so much for thinking of such a personal gift." Annie shook her head. "Caroline, your hair is so beautiful."

"Sometimes I wish it wasn't so long."

"You can have it any length you want." Annie knew full well the patience it took to groom long hair.

Caroline turned around to face her on the bed. "You don't think Uncle Jared would mind if I got it cut? Some of the girls at school got theirs cut to their shoulders and it looks so cool."

Annie reached out and smoothed her knuckles over the little girl's flushed cheek. "Your uncle wouldn't mind," she said.

"Could we get it done tomorrow, after school?"

Annie smiled. "I have that gift certificate to the hair salon that Lewis got me. I'll never use it all. We'll drop the boys off at Grandma's house and then we'll go get hair cuts."

Caroline took the brush from her and nodded as if convincing herself this was what she really wanted to do. "Thanks."

"Hey, I know how much of a pain long hair can be," she said, pulling her braid over her shoulder. "I need some split ends cut, anyway."

Annie waited as Caroline crawled under the covers. "I'll see you in the morning."

The little girl smiled a little as her eyes closed.

When she went downstairs Jared was already hanging the photograph on the wall. "Once the children start hitting their milestones in life we're going to need a bigger wall."

Jared motioned around the room. "We have three others in here…pick any one you like." He came to stand in front of her. "It was nice seeing you so happy tonight. I don't ever want to see you sad."

Sad? How on earth could she ever be sad or unhappy when everything in life she had ever wanted was under this roof? "I'm content, I have a family and I have a kind and decent husband."

He looked embarrassed. "I have a few things to sort through…with myself…my past," he admitted. "But Annie, God knows I want to try."

"Then take your time," she told him. "I'll be here when you decide you're ready."

Chapter Nine

He hugged her so tightly she was about to protest, then decided it was just too nice a feeling and stayed in his arms.

She was still smiling as she left him in the hallway a few minutes later to go to her room. She spread the quilt on the bed, marveling at the beautiful creation.

Tired as she was, she took the time to begin her journal. She sat for a moment putting her thoughts in order and in less than an hour she had written five whole pages. She hesitated writing anything about Toby, about her past and the secret she kept, but this was her journal, and she would put it away safely enough. She couldn't tell this to anyone—share her feelings about being with her son again—but she could put it all on paper.

When she finished, she tucked the journal into the bottom drawer of the big old oak bureau, covering it with clothing. Then she crawled into bed, as always her mind drifting to the man who lay just down the hall. Their relationship was still so new, so fragile in many ways.

The thought that maybe someday they would share a room seemed so out of reach right now. Still, Jared made small steps every day.

Annie had faith in God and trust in Jared. Faith and trust would be enough.

"You don't think it looks gross, do you?"

The hairstylist turned Caroline around to face Annie. She'd watched the process for the last half hour.

The young woman had taken Caroline quite seriously, listening to everything the girl had told her and asking a few questions about what she would prefer.

Then, while having a running conversation with her young client about country music, actors and cool video games, the woman had worked her magic.

Now Caroline sat there, that familiar worried frown on her face. Annie wasn't about to ruin this moment for her with hesitation or anything but praise.

"That cut looks good on you, and the length is perfect."

"Really?" Unsure, the girl reached up to finger the ends that kissed her shoulders. "It feels so different, my head feels so light."

"You had a lot of hair, young lady." Sondra held a mirror in her hands. "Want to see what it looks like from the back?"

Caroline nodded and once again smiled as she took in her new look.

When they went to pick the boys up, Eve, ever supportive and encouraging, raved about the cut. Mick said his little granddaughter was growing up too fast, but he said it with a smile and admitted he liked it. Luke teased her about it in fun and Toby seemed fascinated, constantly looking at Caroline to see where her hair had gone.

But they didn't have to wait too long for the reaction they most wanted. When they arrived home the boys raced out the back door to feed the critters.

Caroline and Annie looked at each other as they heard Jared come in the back door. Caroline was so tense Annie wanted to hug her.

When Jared stopped in the doorway he opened his mouth to speak and then he looked at his niece. Annie prayed he would say the right thing.

Please God, she prayed, *help him to see this is something Caroline feels so sure about, that it's her way of taking control of one little thing.*

Self-consciously, Caroline reached up and tucked her hair behind her ears. "I asked Annie to help me with my hair." Her tone was almost apologetic. "It was just so long."

Jared looked at Annie, his expression not revealing a thing. He walked toward Caroline, kneeling down. "I think it looks pretty. It will certainly be much cooler for you."

The breath Caroline let out was one of relief, then she laughed. "I thought you'd be mad at me for doing it and with Annie for letting me."

He took her hands in his. "Why would I be mad at

either of you? It's your hair. If you want to get it cut, you can. If you want to dye it purple, *then* we'll talk."

Caroline laughed again. "I'm going to call Michelle and tell her." She raced into the living room.

Annie put her handbag on the table as Jared pushed to his feet. "She made the decision last night and asked me if I'd take her."

"I'm glad she has you here. I often wondered how on earth she washed all that hair, anyway. Come to think of it, I wonder the same thing about you."

"There are times when I consider getting it cut," she said, flipping the braid back over her shoulder.

"But you're not going to...right?"

She chuckled. "No."

His relief made her smile. "Good."

"It was your opinion that mattered most to Caroline. That girl would walk through fire before doing anything to disappoint you. You're her hero."

Jared wanted to be Annie's hero. He wanted to be the man who gave her everything she deserved in life.

"There was a message on the machine when I came in earlier." He pulled a rag from his back pocket and wiped his hands.

"Oh?"

"The lady from child welfare. She'll be here Wednesday afternoon. She wants to meet with the children, talk to them and meet you."

Annie had just two days to prepare herself for the most important meeting of her life. "We'll be okay. You're worried, I know."

"Only because I don't know what I'd do if I lost the kids, if they went back into the system."

Annie closed the distance between them, placing her hands on his arms. "We're not going to lose them. She'll see that we are a family."

He looked down into those beautiful green eyes and wondered what it would be like to just let go and lose himself in them, in her.

He was nervous about the social worker coming to evaluate them. Yet when he looked into her eyes, a calm washed over him.

With Annie by his side everything would be okay.

Annie was up earlier than normal two days later. Jared was up and eating breakfast, so she did a few extra loads of laundry before the kids woke. When the doorbell rang, she looked at the clock on the wall. Jared met her at the kitchen door as she came down the hall. "Who could it be at this hour?"

Annie wiped her hands on her jeans and opened the door. The woman who stared back at her through the screen door looked years older than she had the last time Annie had seen her.

Her skin was pale and drawn, and she'd lost weight. Her once bleached-blond hair was now a silvery gray. Her hands trembled as she raised a cigarette to her mouth and took one last puff before throwing it out onto the driveway, where it landed in the dirt.

"Hello, Mum."

She spoke the words in a voice that sounded so much

like that of a child—soft and hesitant. Jared came up behind her and she felt his strength and unspoken support in the arm that went around her shoulder.

"My girl's done all right for herself," said Sylvia. "Aren't you going to invite me in, introduce me to your husband?"

Annie pushed the screen door open and Sylvia came into the hallway, a small handbag over one arm, a suitcase clutched in the other hand.

"Mum, this is Jared Campbell."

She smiled up at him and all Jared could do was wonder what her appearance here was doing to Annie. For his wife's sake, he was gracious.

"I smell coffee. I missed breakfast traveling on the bus."

The hint was not lost on Annie. "Would you like something to eat?"

Sylvia smiled as if she'd won the lottery. "Thought you'd never ask." She found her way down the hall to the kitchen, looking the house over as she went.

"Are you okay?"

Annie shivered slightly. "I don't know how she found out about us. I don't know why she's here. I didn't invite her, Jared."

"I know that." He pulled her into his arms. "This isn't easy for you, and that worries me."

"You don't like her. I sensed that from the times I've spoken of her. I told you she wouldn't be part of our lives."

"It's not that I don't like her, I just don't like the life

she gave you. I hate the fact that you missed out on so much and she should have given you more."

He cared about her, Annie thought, hugging him back. He cared that she'd once been a scared, shy girl. It mattered to him that her mother's presence here was not easy for her.

"I don't believe she had anything to give me after the hatred and bitterness had eaten away at her."

Suddenly a horrifying scenario occurred to her. She pushed back to look up at him. "The social worker comes today!"

He smoothed back tendrils of hair from her forehead and kissed it—a purposeful kiss. "We'll deal with one problem at a time."

They walked to the kitchen to find Sylvia seated at the table with a cup of coffee in her hands. "Hope you don't mind, I helped myself."

Annie found a smile. "Of course not. Would you like something to eat? Some eggs and toast?"

Sylvia settled back in the chair, looking at Annie with eyes that seemed far too calm and cool. Strangely enough, Annie couldn't ever remember those eyes looking warm.

"Sure…that'd be great."

"So, Mrs. Dawson, what brings you back to Guthrie?" Jared asked, refilling his cup before sitting down.

"I keep in touch with a couple of the friends I made at the social club years back and one of them told me my little girl had moved back here and married."

Annie bit her tongue. She knew what pals she'd made at the club—her drinking buddies. She should have known that a few of them still kept in contact with her.

"You never thought to invite me to your wedding? Every mother should have that right, you know."

Annie turned from the stove. She wanted to tell Sylvia that she'd given up any rights of being a mother the day she'd stopped caring about her child.

Instead she chose to let it go. Annie had the life she wanted, far from that awful time that for the past few months had been a mere memory, not a torment.

"I didn't know where you were. And I believe your last words to me were 'do what you want with your life, just don't bother me.'"

"And you took me seriously? Mothers say things they don't mean sometimes."

If she thought about it for a week, Annie would never be able to come up with anything in her life that her mother had said to her and not meant. Sylvia had always chosen her words to do the most damage, to cut closest to the bone.

Annie finished the eggs, cooked the toast and brought the plate to the table, setting it before her mother. Jared held out his hand to her and she sat beside him.

"You've surprised me. Just showing up out of the blue."

"Thought I'd come for a visit. House looks big enough. You shouldn't have a problem finding a room for your old mum."

"You can't stay here." The words tumbled out of her mouth. Jared reached over and took her hand in his, squeezing it. Sylvia looked at her with a stony expression.

"What Annie means is that maybe you'd be more comfortable with your friends in town, that way you'd have transportation and wouldn't be stuck out here all day."

Sylvia frowned. "I know exactly what Annie means. If anyone can carry a grudge, it's my daughter." She looked at Annie. "I did right by you all those years, you know. I didn't have to keep you with me but I did."

Annie couldn't sit here and not speak the truth. "You hated me. You told me that many times. I was a reminder of my father."

"I did not hate you."

"One day after the social worker left I remember what you said to me." She had no trouble recalling the painful memory. "I asked if you wanted me to stay because you loved me. You told me your life was miserable and if you had to suffer, so did I."

Jared didn't know how much more of this he could stand to hear without wanting to remove Sylvia from his house and hug Annie, hug her for all the times this woman hadn't.

He knew about forgiveness, he'd learned about it in church, had tried to practice it in his everyday life, but God tested him sometimes and forgiving was hard.

"I say we should just let it be water under the bridge."

It was at that point, tension in the room so thick it

was claustrophobic, that Luke and Caroline came into the room. Both stopped in the doorway and looked from the stranger to Annie.

"I heard your sister got killed. My friend in town told me you got the kids." She glanced at the children. "Guess that kind of makes me your grandma then."

Luke yawned and went straight to Annie, hugging her. "Can I have some cereal, please?"

"Sure, sweetie, sit down and I'll get it."

Caroline helped herself as always. When she stood near the sink with Annie she touched her arm. "She's not my grandma, is she?" The girl whispered.

Annie bent to place a kiss on the girl's head. "No, honey, she isn't. And don't let her worry or frighten you."

Caroline looked worried just the same. "Don't let her make you sad, Annie."

Breakfast seemed to drag on for an eternity. Sylvia peppered the kids with questions and if she made an enquiry of Jared, he was polite, though his tone was cool.

"Why don't you take the kids to school this morning, Jared?" Annie began clearing the table. "I'll get Toby up and straighten the house."

Jared could tell she wanted time alone with her mother. It was something she felt she had to do. He had to trust her enough to let her do it.

He met her at the sink as the kids left the room to get their backpacks. Placing his hand under her chin, he lifted it until she looked him in the eye.

"You're a strong woman. You've come so far from

the little girl she used to treat so badly. Don't let her drag you back."

She smiled and instinctively hugged him, pleased when his arms came around her in a strong embrace, infusing her with a steel will.

"I'll be fine. She wants something, I'm sure of it. That's the only reason she'd even look for me."

"If you need me for anything I have my cell phone. I'll turn right around and come back if I have to."

"Take the kids to school. I'll be here when you get back." He blew her a kiss from the door, said a polite goodbye to Sylvia and herded the kids out to the truck.

Annie excused herself and went upstairs to get Toby. He was just waking up as she entered the room and she pulled him into her arms. She quickly returned to the kitchen, not wanting to leave her mother alone too long.

"Another one?"

Annie didn't reply to her mother's surprised question. Toby waited for his breakfast, all the while looking at this stranger.

"I heard the parents got killed just after they built this place. Guess even the lucky ones don't get everything."

Annie drew on all her strength, on all God's teachings about forgiveness that had been passed down through the ages. Part of her wanted to believe in the tiny hope that her mother actually might want a relationship with her, might actually be sad at what she had missed.

Her heart knew differently. She came back to the table and gave Toby his bowl of cereal. She looked at her mother, trying to feel something, anything.

She wasn't surprised when she felt nothing at all.

"Why are you here, Mum?"

"I came to see you and—"

"The truth," said Annie. "Just tell me why you came back."

Sylvia took out a cigarette and pulled a lighter from her bag. Annie shook her head and her mother put them down on the table.

"I need money. I figured you married into the Campbell family, you should be able to get your hands on some cash."

Annie didn't know why she felt a spear of hurt go through her. It's not like she hadn't expected something like this.

"I'm not giving you cash so you can drink it away."

Sylvia looked at her with an expression that gave "mean" a whole new definition. "I'm not drinking."

But Annie knew the signs, knew she was lying. The bloodshot eyes, the slight tremor in her hands because she hadn't been able to have a drink since she'd been here.

"If I went to your suitcase now I'd find at least one bottle of Scotch."

"Like you never used anything to get you through the day," she said. "You always did think you were better than me."

"Is that what you think?"

Sylvia crossed her arms and looked genuinely hurt. "Yes. You and that Campbell girl always together, her filling your head with ideas."

"Sara was my friend. She cared about me."

"Guess it made her feel good to befriend the town trash."

It would take restraint, but Annie would get through this and her mother would leave here without making her angry.

"I'd like you to leave. I want you to take your suitcase and your hatred and leave my home."

"You got married and respectable and now you just throw me out?"

Annie stood now as Toby reached his hands up for her. He sensed the tension in the room and was getting frightened.

"I had respectability before I married Jared. I'm not throwing you out, I'm asking you to leave."

The look that crossed the older woman's face was one Annie would remember forever. It was a look of total and absolute surprise.

It was also the moment when, just for a second, Annie wondered if there was even a chance that her mother would change, that she would love the daughter she'd never wanted.

"Please, Annie." It wasn't the words but the tone Sylvia used. In that one short plea Annie heard defeat, as if the woman was finally worn down, having played her last card and lost. "If I could just stay one night."

"Mum—"

"I rode up on the bus, I couldn't sleep. I...thought you'd be happy to see me, but I know better." She wrung her hands in front of her. "I just need a good sleep in a comfortable bed and maybe a home-cooked meal, then tomorrow morning I'll get a ride into town and go back on the bus."

Annie tried to call up every horrid day she'd spent with her mother, tried to recall every mean thing she'd ever said, every uncaring thing she'd ever done, all in the hope she could tell her mother no.

But in her heart, Annie couldn't turn her back on the woman. "I have to talk it over with Jared when he gets back from town," she said. "But there are going to be some ground rules if he says yes."

Her mother nodded, her lips drawn into a thin line.

"When you talk to me, you'll be polite if nothing else. I won't have the children seeing you be mean. And you will respect my husband and my home."

"Agreed."

Annie set Toby on the floor. "Go find the toy box, little man. Build me something with those big blocks."

Toby grinned at her. "Bid bocks."

Annie chuckled. "Close enough."

She started cleaning the table and was more than surprised when her mother got up and started helping. "You don't have to do that."

Her mother gave her a tough look, then tried to soften it with a smile that seemed foreign to her. "I'm not doing it because I have to."

Annie had the sneaking suspicion that she was doing it to help her chances of staying the night, but she didn't comment on it.

"You're good with the children."

"They make it easy."

"I never really had that…ability or whatever you call it."

"It's maternal instinct."

Sylvia shrugged and put the dishes in the sink. "Not every woman has it."

Annie didn't feel like getting into an argument. "I guess not."

When she heard Jared return, she dried her hands, then excused herself and met him at the front door.

"How's it going?"

"I need to talk to you."

Jared put his car keys on the hall table. "Shoot."

"Things got a little heated after you left and I asked her to leave."

"I'll drive her into town."

"She practically begged me to let her stay one night. She said she just wanted a bed and a warm meal." Annie held up her hands. "After all she's done to me through the years, why can't I just say no and tell her to leave?"

Jared pulled her into his arms. "Because she finds it easy to be mean for whatever reason. You, on the other hand, don't have it in you, Annie, not even now."

"I know this comes at a bad time, today being the day the social worker is coming and it's unfair to ask you—"

"She can stay the night if you're comfortable with it," he said. "I'll take her to the bus tomorrow morning with the kids on the way to school."

Annie hugged him. "Thank you so much."

"You're welcome." He paused then said, "There is one thing you probably haven't thought of."

"What?"

"She's going to draw conclusions when she sees that we sleep in separate rooms, Annie. And if we can't find a way to get her out of here this afternoon for a few hours, she might let it slip in front of the social worker."

Annie looked stricken. "I didn't even think!"

"It's okay. Move some things into my room today. I'll set up a makeshift bed on the floor tonight and you can have the bed. We'll lock the door in case she comes snooping."

"That might work. I'll go tell her she can stay."

"Annie?"

She turned. "Yes?"

"You know I want everything with you."

She smiled. "I know."

"I'm just so used to using the past, it's hard to let go and trust something I've never trusted before."

"Love?"

"Yeah."

"I'm already there," she confessed, noting his surprise. "I'll wait for you as long as it takes because there isn't anyone else I'd rather share it with."

When she was gone, Jared stood there for a long time, listening to hushed voices in the kitchen. Hearing movement in the living room, he walked to the doorway and smiled as he watched Toby. The child's face was a study in concentration as he tried to build a tower with the plastic building blocks Annie had bought him.

Jared recalled the fear he'd felt when the awesome responsibility of looking after these kids had been left to him. He'd never once considered not doing it. This was something he could do for Sara and James. Now it was his mission in life.

The children had each brought something unique into his life. Their love soothed parts of him that had been scarred so badly he didn't ever think they would heal. And those gaping chasms in his heart carved by years of first neglect, then abandonment, at the hands of his mother, they were starting to heal, too.

The soothing balm for them had been the kindness and love of a red-haired wonder with the softest smile he'd ever seen, green eyes that warmed him and a heart that didn't know how to be anything but loving.

He was ready to let go of those old chains that held him prisoner. Annie had proven herself to be someone he could trust not only with his family, but also with his heart.

By the time Annie left to get the kids from school, Jared had spent the better part of the day puttering around inside the house. He didn't seek out a conversation with Sylvia and after a few attempts at trying to draw him out, she gave up and asked if it would be all right to call her friend in town. Annie had mentioned her reservations to Jared about leaving her mother in the house alone and he had promised to keep a close eye on her.

When she pulled into the school yard Caroline and

Luke came running to the car, smiles on their faces, their cheeks rosy with life.

The little girl jumped in the front and Luke climbed in beside his brother. "Everyone liked my hair, Annie. They thought it was so grown-up." Caroline bubbled over like a sparkling cider. "And if feels so much better!"

"That's wonderful, sweetie. I'm glad you like it."

"And guess what, Annie?" Luke squirmed with excitement. "I got a gold star for my reading and Billy brought a really big lizard to school today for show and tell."

"I'm very proud of your gold star, Luke. Wait until we tell Uncle Jared. As for the lizard, I'm sure Billy's mum was happy to have it gone for the day."

"Nah, she doesn't mind. He's just not s'posed to bring it in the house."

"Is your mother still at home?" Caroline asked.

"She's staying just for tonight, sweetie. In the morning she's leaving on the bus."

As they drove home Caroline turned the radio on and soon they were all singing, slightly out of key, to a popular song.

Life didn't get any better than this. All her dreams were coming true, her prayers answered. She had the ingredients of a contented life—family, commitment, love.

Even this visit with her mother had helped her to put to rest once and for all the slim hope she'd harbored that someday they would have a relationship.

Annie saw the small black car parked under a shady tree when they got home. She ushered the children inside, Toby chasing after his siblings as fast as his legs would carry him. She heard voices before she ever reached the living room. When she appeared in the doorway Jared was seated in one chair and a pleasant-looking woman in her thirties sat across from him.

Jared stood when he saw her. "Annie." He said her name with a relief the other woman probably didn't notice…but *she* did. "Mrs. Keller arrived early."

Annie smiled at the woman and whispered to Jared. "Mum?"

"The Lord is working overtime for us today. One of her friends came and picked her up. She'll be back sometime tonight."

At least with her mother out of the house, Annie didn't have to worry about anything catastrophic going wrong with this visit.

She just hoped her mother didn't come home drunk.

Annie held out her hand and the woman took it, rising from the chair with a friendly smile. "Nice to meet you, Mrs. Keller."

"Please, call me Trish. And it's a pleasure to finally meet you. I'm sorry if my early arrival has caused problems for you."

"Of course not. In fact, I'm just going to get the children their afternoon snack before they settle in for homework if you'd like to join us."

The woman surveyed Annie with wise eyes. "I'd like that very much."

Annie ran her hand down Jared's arm as she walked by, squeezing his hand in a gesture of support. He wondered, not for the first time, what he'd done to deserve this woman. He followed them into the kitchen and helped Annie prepare food and juice.

"I can make you a cup of tea or coffee if you'd prefer it."

"That juice looks awfully good. I get a little sick of coffee all the time. It will be a refreshing change."

Minutes later, the kitchen was filled with chatter as the kids came downstairs. Toby always missed his brother and sister during the day so when they came home he followed them around like a shadow. Caroline stopped in the doorway, her worried glance going from the woman she remembered to Annie and then Jared.

"Kids, this is Mrs. Keller. She came to visit just after I moved in here with you." Jared skirted the issue of their parents' death. "Annie's got your snacks ready."

Caroline couldn't keep the fear out of her eyes. Annie hadn't seen that in the past few weeks as the girl had come more and more out of herself. Now she ate silently, sipping her juice, all the while her eyes on Trish. Luke wasn't nearly so intimidated.

"You're the lady who said we couldn't stay with Uncle Jared if he didn't have a wife." The boy's smile expanded. "He's got Annie now so we can stay."

Chapter Ten

In this little boy's mind that was an end to it. She had set down rules. Jared had met them. Annie wished it were that simple.

"That's why I came here today, Luke. To talk to you all, see how things are working out here."

"Things are great," he said around a mouthful of cracker and cheese. He swallowed before continuing. "Annie can cook and she knows how to fish. And when she reads my bedtime stories she does different voices for all the people."

Trish smiled and Annie got the impression it was a genuine gesture. "Wow...fishing...I can see where that would be important."

Luke nodded. "It is."

Toby chose that moment to crawl onto Jared's knee and reached for a cup Annie had put out for him.

"One thing I did notice is how lived-in the house looks."

Jared frowned. "Lived-in?"

"Usually people are so worried that they straighten everything to look like a drill sergeant's army barracks. Personally I like to see a house with some clutter—it shows that people treat it as a home, a haven."

Annie chuckled. "Clutter we can do on just about any given day."

"Oh, I'm sure." She then proceeded to ask the children questions. Annie was pleased to find they weren't intrusive questions.

This woman knew how to phrase her inquiries in a way that was at once friendly and curious. There wasn't a hint of interrogation or procedure about it.

When Caroline was asked a question she looked to Annie.

Not knowing what else to do, Annie smiled. "Sweetie, don't be scared. Mrs. Keller is here to help. She really wants to know what you think and how you feel about everything."

After that, it didn't seem so much like pulling teeth to get answers from her. Both the children were very forthright and some of the answers were childishly sweet. Luke told her he was learning to read better. Caroline divulged that Annie was her friend and that she made her uncle happy.

Finally, Trish got to what Annie hoped was the end of her visit. She turned first to Luke. "What do you like best about living here?"

He shrugged and looked at the table for a long time. Finally, on a heavy sigh, he looked back at her.

"Uncle Jared loves me. So does Annie. They love all of us."

It was Caroline who said it best. "We're a family."

Trish closed her notebook. "Yes, you are." She stood, putting the notebook in her handbag. "I think that's all I need here today."

Annie and Jared stood to follow her out. Jared set Toby on his chair. "You guys finish up here so you can start on homework."

They walked Trish to the front door. She turned on the threshold. Annie felt Jared slip his hand into hers and squeeze tight.

"Mr. Campbell, I'd like to be honest."

Jared cleared his throat and prepared for the worst. "You should be."

"I had the distinct feeling when I visited last time you didn't have a fiancée, nor were you planning to get married."

When he would have objected, she held up a hand. "Please let me finish. The reasons why you got married don't concern me. Some of my colleagues would disagree, but that's my opinion and in this instance mine is the only opinion that counts.

"You can tell a lot by talking candidly with children, even young children. They have a habit of telling it just like it is."

"We encourage the children to say what is on their mind."

"A wise decision. I'm impressed by what I've seen here today and by what I've heard. I'll be making my recommendation to my superiors and I should be in touch in a few days."

Jared wanted to scream. A few days was just more torture. They had already waited long enough, in this limbo. "We'll wait for your call."

She turned to walk out the door, stopped and looked back one last time. "In my line of work I see a lot of houses, big beautiful houses, with carefully kept lawns and matching interior decorations. But I don't see many *homes.*"

She smiled at Annie. "Mrs. Campbell, you have a lovely home."

Annie couldn't help the glow of pride she felt. "Thank you."

As Mrs. Keller drove away, Jared hugged Annie. "How do you think it went?"

"I think in a few years you're going to be putting the fear of God into the boys Caroline brings home and helping Luke buy his first car."

"I couldn't have done it without you."

Annie smiled with pleasure at his statement. "I'm going to invite your parents for dinner. Do you think they'll mind that Mum is here?"

"They'll treat her like a friend they haven't seen in years."

And true to Jared's word, Eve and Mick were as gracious and friendly as she had come to know them to be. Sylvia arrived home just before dinner.

"Were you nervous, son?" asked Mick.

"I was. We had a lot at stake."

Eve sent her son a supportive smile. "From what you've told me, Mrs. Keller seems a very reasonable woman. I'm sure her recommendation will be in your favor."

"Never did have time for no welfare people when I lived here." Sylvia's statement was blunt. "Annie, you remember how they used to come poking their nose into our business?"

Oh, Annie remembered. But it was pointless to try and make Sylvia see how much better off her daughter would have been going to live with strangers.

"Luke, why don't you tell Grandma about the gold star you got today?" she said, ending a conversation far too solemn for the dinner table.

Luke didn't need any more encouragement than that. He went into the whole story, told only the way an imaginative child can do.

Later in the evening with Sylvia outside for a cigarette and Jared and Mick in the living room with the children, Eve helped Annie with the dishes.

"How are you holding up with your mother here?"

"I asked her to leave earlier today because she upset me. Then when she pleaded with me to let her stay just for tonight, I couldn't turn her away."

"She's your mother."

"She never wanted to be."

"You have an inner strength, Annie. I see it in every thing you do, with Jared, with the children." She hugged her tight. "Thank you for making my son smile again."

"He makes it easy, believe me."

That night Annie stood outside the room she was about to share with Jared. She could hear him moving around. Was he nervous? Did he realize what a huge step this was and how many little steps—not to mention obstacles—they'd had to pass to get here?

When the door suddenly opened, Annie felt a blush rise in her cheeks. He held out his hand to her. She took it and he pulled her into the room.

Jared closed the door and turned to face her. "Annie, I'd like to sleep beside you tonight. I'll understand if you would prefer me on the floor but I'm hoping you'll say yes."

Annie had always believed actions spoke louder than words. She walked to the bed, picked up the nightgown she had laid out earlier and looked back at him.

"Small steps, Jared, that's all you have to take. And yes, I would be honored to take this step with you."

She disappeared into the bathroom adjoining his room and Jared used the time to change into pajama bottoms, his usual night attire. In deference to Annie and this being their first time sleeping together, he threw a loose-fitting T-shirt on, as well.

When she came out of the bathroom he caught his breath at the vision that was his wife. With her hands clasped in front of her, she was the sweetest thing he had ever seen. She'd taken her hair out of its braid and now it hung down her back, brushed and shiny to her waist.

The nightgown was demure, like Annie herself. It was cotton and lace, very plain in its design. Jared knew on any other woman it would look plain. Not on Annie.

On her it looked as sweet and innocent as she was. It was simple and fine. And it was the sexiest creation he could imagine.

That amazed him. It covered her to mid-calf and yet was all the more sensual because of it.

"Jared, you're looking at me like you've never seen me before." He was staring at her with eyes that made her feel he was touching her.

"I think as long as I live there will be sides to you that I discover along the way."

Annie had feasted on the sight of him, too. He was handsome in a suit and tie sitting in church. He was rugged when outside, dirty and dusty with grease smudges everywhere.

But in his soft cotton bottoms and a grey shirt that bore the name of the college he and Lewis had attended, he looked so good, so attractive and touchable, that Annie was thankful he was her husband, that no other woman would ever see him like this again.

When they crawled into bed Annie lay on her side, facing away from him. She wondered at first if he would take that as a cue that she didn't want to be near him, so she scooted more into the middle of the bed and waited.

He turned out the light and slid in behind her. The mattress sank with his weight. He laid himself against her spoon fashion, sliding his arm around her slowly.

Annie nestled into him, an action that had Jared almost groaning with the restraint it took to keep the pace steady, to take things slow this first night together.

If her mother wasn't in the house, and the tensions of the day hadn't left them both drained, they would have become intimate tonight.

It would not have been awkward, but a natural progression of what they had both been journeying toward.

"I'm sorry I'm so tense." She tried to move away in embarrassment. He held her firm and she stopped wriggling.

"Don't be sorry. There is no right or wrong at this, Annie." The words were whispered in her ear. "Small steps, remember? Just relax and sleep."

So she did. Annie lay there in the arms of a man she had fallen hopelessly in love with. She lay there and sent a prayer of thanks to heaven as she did every night.

But this night was special. This night she had found more with Jared than she could ever have imagined on that first day in the restaurant.

Tomorrow, when her mother was gone, she was going to tell him her secret. It would test the strength of their union, of the feelings he had for her.

And even though it was still as big a risk as it always had been, even though she could lose everything, Annie trusted her husband. She trusted the feelings he shared with her, the kindness he showed to her and the love she could feel building between them.

No more lies, she told herself resolutely, no more guilt. Tomorrow she would tell him and they could deal with it. It might take him a while but she would wait.

She could feel his strong heartbeat rapping out a

rather quick cadence. She turned her head so she could see his silhouette, feel his soft breath on her face.

"Good night, Jared."

She hadn't expected it, but when he kissed her it was the most natural thing in the world. It was a kiss of promise, a kiss of intention on his part.

It was a deeper kiss than they had shared before and it left Annie tingling from her head to her toes and left her so aware of her whole body and of his.

When the kiss finally ended he pulled her closer. "'Night, Annie."

Annie woke the next morning and dressed while Jared was still in the shower. Everything she did this morning had a zing to it. Even tying her tennis shoes made her smile. Not the action itself, but the sheer joy she felt at having spent the night in Jared's arms. The effects of his kiss still lingered, a very potent mix that she knew she would get used to without any trouble at all.

Today she felt she could take on the world with one arm tied behind her back and come out on top. When she walked into the kitchen she was surprised to see her mother sitting at the table, a cup of coffee in front of her.

"Good morning, Mum."

"Yes, it is." Her tone was unusually bright and cheerful. "I'll be leaving as soon as your husband can get me into town and I'll be taking whatever cash you have."

"Mum, I told you yesterday, I'll buy you food vouchers or anything you need to help you out, but I'm not giving you cash."

"Really?" She reached into her handbag and pulled out a leather-bound book. Annie thought her heart would stop beating.

She'd hidden the journal in Jared's room last night, folded among her things. Never in her wildest dreams would she have thought her mother would invade her privacy to that degree.

"I think you'll find me the cash I need. Unless you want me to tell your little secret."

"You went through my things…you went into the room I shared with my husband!"

Sylvia didn't even look ashamed. "Last night when you were outside talking to his parents before they left. I wanted money but this is a lot more valuable."

Annie made a move to the table but Sylvia snatched the book up. "Mum, please." Annie's voice was no louder than a whisper, tears welling in her eyes. "I need to tell Jared in my own way."

"Tsk tsk, Annie, keeping secrets from your husband is just not a good foundation for a lasting marriage."

Annie stood up to her mother like never before. "I won't give in to your blackmail. I won't let you do this to me or my family."

Sylvia shrugged. "Good for you. It should be interesting to see the look on Jared's face when I tell him Toby is your son."

Annie turned, planning to march right up the stairs and tell Jared herself, but it was too late. He stood in the doorway staring at her. The expression on his face would stay with Annie the rest of her life. The hurt and disbelief she saw there told her the perfect world she'd woken up to had just shattered into a million pieces.

"Jared—"

He held up his hands. "We'll talk later, Annie." His tone was cold and distant, as if he were speaking to a stranger. Then he turned his attention on Sylvia.

"Nobody comes in here and threatens my family." He was fierce, walking over and taking the journal from her.

Sylvia actually shrank back, suddenly scared of the man who towered over her.

"Get your suitcase, Mrs. Dawson. I'm taking you into the bus station, and if you have an ounce of common sense you won't say one word between here and there."

He glanced at Annie, as if he couldn't bear to look at her for more than a few seconds. "You can drop the kids at school this morning if I'm not back."

Sylvia didn't say another word to Annie, just gave her a glare and followed him out the door. Her mother was walking out of her life leaving a trail of heartbreak behind her.

As soon as she heard the truck idle down the driveway and fade into the distance, Annie picked up the telephone with trembling fingers and dialed Lewis's home number.

"Annie? I know you guys get up early in the country but this is ridiculous," Lewis said with a chuckle.

"Jared knows about Toby."

"What happened?" he asked, all the humor gone from his voice.

When she finished recounting the story, Lewis sighed heavily. "Ah, kid, I'm sorry."

"I had made up my mind last night to tell him this morning." She didn't go into details of how the relationship had progressed.

"I just don't know what he's going to do, what he's going to say. After he found out he just looked at me…like he couldn't bear to be near me."

"I'm going to clear my schedule for the end of the week and come up. I'd leave today but I'm waiting on a ruling in a case."

"I know I should have told him sooner but I can't lose what I've found here."

"You're in love with him."

"More than I ever knew love could be. And Jared was starting to trust his feelings for me. Now he hates me."

"He's angry and he's hurt, Annie. He feels betrayed but he doesn't hate you." And by the time the phone call ended she was clinging to the hope that Jared didn't hate her.

When the children came down Annie found a sliver of calm. She couldn't let them know anything was wrong. Her stomach churned and her hands shook but she managed.

"Did Uncle Jared already go out into the fields?" asked Caroline.

Annie handed her a glass of milk. "No, he took my

mother into the bus station," she said. "I'll be dropping you at school today."

After that Annie moved around the kitchen like an automaton. Her mind whirled, the life she'd made here looked to be teetering on the brink of destruction. And there was nothing she could do but wait until he came back, until he was ready to talk about it. Annie felt she was on borrowed time.

When she got back from dropping the children off, his truck was parked in the garage. On legs that threatened to quit on her she walked inside.

He was sitting in the living room, her journal beside him on the table and a photograph held in his hands. When he put it down on the table she saw it was the one he had given her for her birthday.

"Where's Toby?"

"I dropped him off at your mother's. I didn't think he needed to be here for this."

"So my mother knows?"

Annie shook her head. "I didn't tell her." Then she said the only thing she could think to say. "I'm sorry, Jared."

His expression was that of a man whose very world had been torn apart. The torment in his eyes hurt her more than his anger ever could have.

"Sorry for what, Annie? Sorry for deceiving me, for using Lewis to help you do it? Or are you sorry that your secret is out?"

Annie sat down. Though her whole body trembled now, she met his hardened gaze and did not look away. She owed him that much.

"I didn't mean to deceive you, and Lewis was involved from the day he handled Toby's adoption. He put me in touch with Sara again."

"My sister knew Toby was your son?"

Annie nodded. "I would have trusted her with my life. I knew she would give Toby everything I couldn't."

"Were you ever going to tell me?"

"Jared, I tried, that first day in the elevator when you dropped me home. I was trying to find a way to tell you and then you let me know in very clear terms what you thought of women who give up their children."

He remained silent and she struggled on, her tone pleading. "Then after last night...I had made up my mind to tell you today, after Sylvia left. I never got the chance."

"You had plenty of chances." It was an accusation, not a statement. "You became part of our family, you made everything seem perfect. I thought you did it out of love for the children, out of your friendship for Sara."

"I did it for all those reasons." The tears rolled down her cheeks but she ignored them. "And I did it because I felt God was giving me the chance to be a mother to Toby again."

Jared stood now and began to pace, agitation in every step. "God gave you that chance when you gave birth to Toby."

"And my circumstances prevented me from keeping him," she said firmly, not allowing the hurt and recrimination in the room make her feel like she had done the wrong thing.

"Sara and James did all the hard work and you just moved in to reap the benefits of their love?"

"No," she said softly, the fight gone from her. There was no reasoning with him, not now. He was hurting. "You were the one who needed help. I did this as much for you as for me."

"And why was that? Did the guilt about giving him up get a little too much to bear?"

"Jared, please think about what you're saying."

"Oh, I know exactly what I'm saying. And I realize now just how special Chris was to you. You were lovers."

Annie accepted the sting of his words. So that, too, was needling at him. It was her past. Everybody had one. She could not erase her past and would not deny it to him or anyone, not anymore.

"Did you ever really care for any of us? Or was it all just part of the charade, part of the plan?"

Annie felt that accusation like a knife through the heart. "You can ask me that after all I went through with Caroline? After the things I shared with you? If that's what you think, then you really don't know me at all."

"You're absolutely right about that. And here I was starting to…" He paused and closed his eyes. "I was starting to let myself love you, trust you. What a joke that was."

"It wasn't a joke. I'm the same woman you slept with last night, I'm the same woman you married."

He pulled her out of the chair, his hands on her arms. "But you aren't. Don't you see that, Annie? It was all built on a lie."

"It was a secret, not a lie."

He let her go as if she burned him. "You *lied*. Were you planning to take him and run off someday? Or maybe file for divorce and use your leverage to take him?"

"Jared, that's unfair."

His laugh was filled with scorn. "Don't talk to me about unfair, Annie, not right now."

She held up her hands in defeat. "So where do we go from here? Do you want me to leave?"

"I'm not putting the children through more upheaval. As much as you've turned my life upside down with your little secret, I won't let you do the same to them."

"Jared, I would never hurt the children."

"What a pity you don't feel the same sensitivity where I'm concerned."

If he wanted a way out, Annie would give it to him. "Do you want a divorce?"

"I don't know what I want right now except some breathing room, time to think."

She left the room abruptly, returning with her purse and her key ring. "I'm going to pick up Toby."

When she closed the front door and walked to the car Annie felt like it wasn't the only door closing on her.

Eve met her at the door when she pulled into their driveway. "Oh, Annie, you've been crying." She pulled her into loving arms and hugged her. "Come on. Let's go inside and you can tell me what's going on."

"How is Toby?"

"He's out back with his grandfather," she said. "But right now we're going to concentrate on you."

Eve sat her down at the table and deposited a box of tissues in front of her, along with a plate of chocolate chip cookies and a glass of milk.

"I think my marriage is over."

Just saying the words sent a chill up her spine.

Eve pulled out a chair and sat down. "Tell me everything."

And so Annie poured out the story, beginning the day she'd left town as a teenager. She didn't leave anything out. The words tumbled out of her mouth and she relived it as she told about the poverty, the menial jobs and shelters she had sometimes stayed in.

She told Eve about Chris, about the love they had found and the situation she found herself in when he died. She told her how she had sworn Sara to secrecy, never wanting any gossip to reflect on Toby or his family.

Finally she blew her nose and took a deep ragged breath.

"I gave up my child and as far as Jared's concerned, I ought to be taken out in the town square and flogged."

"Annie, that man wouldn't hurt a hair on your head and he'd battle anyone who tried to harm you."

"He hates me!"

"I don't think he does. Adoption just happens to be a sore spot with him."

"What would he have preferred I do? Keep Toby and risk becoming a bitter, neglectful mother like Sylvia or his own mother?" Annie realized too late what she'd said. "Eve, I'm sorry...I didn't mean to imply you weren't his mother—"

Eve took her hand. "I've been as much of a mother to Jared as he ever let me be. Don't get me wrong. I love him and I'm as proud of him as any mother could be."

She shook her head. "But all the love Mick and I gave him was never enough to wipe away the scars left by his biological mother. Until he faces the past he's always tried to forget, he isn't ever going to be free of it."

"I don't know how things will be at the house now. Not with Jared so upset. He can barely bring himself to talk to me let alone be in the same room with me."

"If things get too unbearable you can always come here."

"I want to be there for the children, at least until Jared decides to throw me out."

"I raised an intelligent son. No matter how upset he is right now, he'll calm down and think about things. He won't throw you out, simply because he wouldn't know what to do without you."

Eve gave her a shrewd look. "He may be willing to cut off his nose to spite his face but isn't going to do that with the children and their relationship with you."

"I don't want my marriage to be over. I don't want to lose Jared."

Eve brushed the hair back from Annie's damp cheeks. "My son is in love with you."

"I think he was slowly getting there before all this. I'm in love with him."

"He'll come around. He just needs to work through this, heal his wounded pride a little. Trust me."

Annie had to trust something. Her whole world was

falling apart and all she could do was cling to the fragments of her life, now shattered in pieces around her.

Please, Lord, help Jared see everything I've done has been out of love.

That afternoon it was a frantic Jared who arrived on his mother's doorstep. "I thought you'd bang down the door!" she said.

"Have you seen Annie?"

"She picked the children up from school and took them for ice cream, then she's taking them home to fix dinner."

"Son, I think you'd better come in and sit awhile," his father added.

"Dad, I have to get back to—"

"No." Mick's tone left no room for argument. "Whatever it is can wait. Nothing is more important than what is going on in your life right now."

"Your father's right."

He followed his father to the screened patio in the back of the house. "Mother, bring us some coffee, would you, sweetheart?"

Eve kissed her husband's cheek. "Coming right up."

Mick settled himself in his favorite chair. "Your mother filled me in this afternoon on what happened. Are you angry that Annie had a man in her life, that she was intimate with him before she knew you?"

Jared didn't even want to examine those feelings, not yet. The ramifications of Toby's birth—and conception—were just starting to sink in.

"You raised me with the teachings of the church, the Commandments. She lied to me, it's as simple as that."

Mick shook his head. "Life is never that simple and the Lord taught a lot about forgiveness."

His father was right but he couldn't find a way through this torment. "You've seen her with Toby. How could she have that kind of contact with her own son and never acknowledge him?"

"Maybe she was just thankful for the fact she had him in her life again."

"Then she shouldn't have given him away."

Mick turned to face his son. "You would have deprived your sister and James of the joy that baby brought them?"

"That's not what I—"

"You would have deprived your mother and me of the happiness we've shared watching him grow and being a part of his life?"

"No. I wouldn't give Toby up for anything."

Mick nodded. "Now imagine how it felt for someone as loving and caring as Annie to be in the position to have to give him up."

"She made the choice." He just couldn't understand how she'd done it. How could she have handed her baby away? "She had other options available to her."

"Are you sure you want to sit in judgment? That is a right the Lord reserves for Himself alone."

Eve appeared with coffee. She handed a cup to her husband and the other to Jared. "Her love for the children wasn't a lie. Her love for you wasn't a lie."

"If she loved me, she wouldn't have lied to me." And if he convinced himself of that, it would make it that much easier to push her out of his life…just the way he'd always done when someone got too close.

"Jared, that girl doesn't know how *not* to love. She could have turned her mother away yesterday, after all that woman put her through growing up…most people would have."

Jared wished he'd never set eyes on Sylvia. He wished he'd just told Annie to send her away. He wanted his life back the way it had been last night.

"Tell me one thing. Did Sara tell either of you about Annie being Toby's mother?"

It was Eve who answered. "No. She never did."

Jared pushed to his feet. "How could Annie give up her child?"

"Did you ask her?"

"This morning. She said she couldn't keep him…I didn't feel like listening too much after that," he admitted.

Eve went to stand in front of her son, waiting until he looked down at her. "Jared, you need to sit down sometime and ask her about her life when she left this town. You need to listen, really hear her."

Jared caught something in his mother's tone. "She told you, didn't she?"

"Yes, she did. And I love that girl just as much today as I did the day she married you and brought sunshine back into all our lives and a smile back to your face."

"Tell me."

"If you want to know, if she truly means that much to you, then you need to ask *her* about it."

He fished the keys out of his pocket. "I have to go." They followed him outside. Just before he drove off, his mother touched his shoulder through the open truck window.

"I know it's hard for you right now. I also know there is a lot of that boy still in you, the boy we first met who was so angry at his mother for not loving him."

Jared didn't say a word, just stared straight ahead. He remembered that boy. The anger he'd felt back then had surfaced today, threatening to suffocate him.

"You need to let him go, Jared. Let him go so you can get on with your life. Learn to trust again, learn to let love in and be happy."

Jared played her words over in his head as he drove home, wondering what would be waiting for him when he got there.

Chapter Eleven

Annie heard the truck pull into the yard. She called for the kids to get washed up for dinner and her directive was met with good-natured groans as they were dragged from the television.

"Dinner's ready," she said, when he appeared in the doorway.

He nodded once and left the room. Annie knew whatever damage had been done to their relationship was permanent. He'd barely even looked at her. She would hold it together for the children and she would keep things as normal as she could. When they all sat down and joined hands to say grace, Jared let her hand go as soon as Luke finished his simple offering.

Just last night their hands had lingered, linked, fingers brushing, skin sliding.

He was leaving her by degrees. Her fear was that soon she would have no place here, that he would leave her to the point where living with him in this house would be unbearable for them all.

The children kept the conversation going tonight and Jared was glad of that. Caroline seemed excited about the school play. Annie promised to take her shopping on the weekend for fabric and a pattern for her costume.

Things seemed so normal on the outside. Nobody would guess that inside he was a cauldron of turmoil and he could tell from the look on Annie's face that she was feeling the strain. He tried not to feel sorry for her; after all, it was her lies that had brought them to this place. She had risked everything by not telling him the truth.

All day he had prayed to God for understanding, for peace, for a way to hurdle this obstacle and salvage what he could of his world.

Now he sat here, not having said a word to Annie since walking through the door. His heart broke a little more with every hour that passed. For a while it had seemed like he'd finally found someone to trust with his heart, his life and his happiness.

In one horrible morning, he had lost it all.

"Jared?"

He'd been so deep in thought he hadn't even heard her come out onto the porch. "What is it?"

She sat down on the step beside him, keeping her distance. "I can handle you knowing about Toby, I can even manage with you being angry at me. What I can't do every day is watch you act like a caged animal when you have to be in the same room with me."

"I don't act like that."

"Yes, you do. If it were just you and me in this house I would weather it, because I think what we found when we weren't looking is better than what most people discover when they search a lifetime."

Was he hearing her? Did she believe him? His dark expression didn't change. "I'd stay because in my heart I know I didn't do anything wrong giving Toby up, and nobody, except maybe your sister, knows how difficult it was for me."

Jared looked across at her, his face shadowed in the moonlight. "He's *your* son, *your* baby. You gave birth to him."

"Yes, I did," she said, proud of the fact that he was the best part of her. "I carried him inside me and felt him moving. I tried convincing myself for eight months that I could give him a good life."

"You could have given him a mother who cared about him."

"But I did. Your sister was a wonderful mother to Toby." She stood up and breathed the fresh night air. "The way you were with me tonight at dinner, unable to look at me, unwilling to speak to me…if this is how it's going to be, then it isn't good for the children for me to be here."

Jared wanted to scream at the top of his lungs. No matter the lie she'd told, no matter how wounded he felt, she was still the best thing for the children.

Pride kept him silent.

"Think it over tonight and let me know. I can always move in with your parents until you decide if I'm still the person you want helping you raise the children."

He stood up, too, frustration in every movement he made. "Annie, I just don't know how to feel about this."

"I'm sorry I lied to you, by omission or any other way. I wanted this so badly—a family, a home." She wanted to reach for him but dared not. "I'm sorry your mother abandoned you. I wish your childhood could have been different."

"Yeah, well, I stopped wishing that a long time ago."

"But you didn't stop running, and you didn't stop hurting. I'm not perfect, Jared, I've made mistakes in my life. But Toby isn't one of them, and neither was giving him up."

He sat there long after she'd gone inside, thoughts and emotions going around in his brain. Tonight he should have been in her arms.

Instead he would be wrapped in the anger and hurt he had carried with him for so long. Once it had been a strange comfort, a reason for keeping his emotions locked up and for keeping people out.

Now he needed more.

By the time he knocked on Caroline's door that night, Jared was tired to the bone, weary to his soul. She sat in bed, the covers pulled up to her waist, holding the photograph he had given Annie on her birthday.

"I like this picture," she said, tracing the figures in it with her fingers.

He sat down on the bed. "I know you don't understand everything that's going on but—"

"Toby is Annie's little boy."

"How do you know that?"

She looked embarrassed. "I went downstairs to get a drink of water and I heard you talking outside. I didn't mean to listen. It just happened."

"When she came in to tell you good night, did you let Annie know you'd heard?"

Caroline shook her head. "I didn't want her to be more upset." She looked at him. "Is that why you don't love her anymore? Because she had a baby?"

He reached out and brushed a finger down her cheek.

"Annie didn't tell me she had a baby," he said, planning to keep this conversation simple and in terms his niece could understand. "When I found out, I was surprised."

"It hurt you, didn't it?"

"Yes." She looked troubled.

"If you've got questions I'll try to answer them as best I can."

Caroline looked directly at him. "Annie gave us Toby. Was that wrong?"

Jared wondered how children were able to cut through all the flotsam of life and nail the heart of the situation. "No. In fact, it made your parents happy."

"I know. Annie came here and looked after us. She was nice to me even when I was mean. If she hurt you, I know she didn't mean to."

"It isn't that simple, Possum."

She looked straight at him. "It should be when you love someone." She looked down at the photograph. "It must have been hard for Annie to give her baby away."

And for the first time, with those few innocent words from a little girl, Jared felt the tears well up in his eyes.

"It wasn't hard for Janice to give me away. And she didn't even try to find someone nice to take me, she just put me in a home."

My mother, too, he thought, surprised at how the silent voice let loose those words in his head.

"That's how I know Annie really loved Toby when he was born," she said. "She found people who would love him as much as she did."

Jared's throat was clogged with emotion and he was grateful when Caroline said good-night and snuggled into bed.

When he left her room, shutting out the light and closing the door, Jared prowled around the house, walking from room to room, looking for the comfort this home had offered him before.

Now he found nothing that even felt like comfort or solace, and upstairs lay a woman who had chiseled a place in his heart that would never be filled by another.

Through everything today, the anger, hurt and frustration…even the betrayal he had felt, he couldn't reconcile the Annie he had come to love with the woman he was trying to convince himself she was. She wasn't the one who had abandoned her child. It was *his* mother who had done that, *his* mother who had kept him until she could no longer bear the sight of him.

She had hurt him, not Annie.

He'd ignored it, refused to think about it and tried to

banish it from his life. Now it was all too clear. Annie wasn't the one who had to leave.

He had to leave and find the rest of himself, the part he'd left inside that little boy long ago. If he didn't find it, if he couldn't offer her the whole of himself, then he would let her go.

He quickly wrote a note and propped it in the middle of the kitchen table for her. He went into the den and made two phone calls, one to his mother and one to Lewis.

Then he packed a bag.

Jared glanced at his watch as he cut the engine in the truck. He had stopped outside the little white house with yellow trim and a garden full of flowers.

Again he checked the address Lewis had gotten for him. This wasn't what he'd expected. The city was still waking up, a paperboy was doing his rounds and here and there a car engine started, the early birds off to work. He would never swap country living to come back here again. The country was home to him.

He walked through the gate and approached the house, not sure of what to feel, wondering if this was a huge mistake and knowing that if it was, he needed to make it.

He rang the doorbell and an elderly man came to the door, his hair gray, his uniform proclaiming he worked for the postal service.

"Can I help you?"

Jared was sure he had the wrong house now. "I'm

looking for Gloria Monahan, but I must have got the address mixed up."

The man looked him up and down. "No. This is where she lives. I'm her husband. The name's Ralph. And you would be?"

"Her son."

His face didn't register surprise; in fact, he hardly reacted at all. "Guess you'd better come in then." He swung the door wide and Jared followed him.

"Glory...someone here to see you."

Ralph disappeared down the hall and Jared heard his mother's voice for the first time in more than twenty years.

She stopped when she saw him, her mouth open, her eyes wide. She pulled the robe tighter around her and smoothed a hand over hair that hadn't yet been brushed into place.

"Jared." His name was spoken on a breath of incredulity.

"It's been a long time."

She eyed him warily. "I often wondered if I'd ever see you again."

"I won't stay too long."

"Good, because Ralph isn't the kind who likes my past dragged up."

He was just that...her past. As he sat on the couch she took the chair across from him. "You look well."

"We're adults, Jared, you can tell it like it is. I look old."

She had aged, and the years had not been kind to her.

Still he couldn't imagine the drinking and smoking had done her many favors.

"Why did you come?"

"I wanted to see you."

"Any particular reason?"

"I needed to put some things to rest," he said. "Old ghosts."

"Excuse me," she said, getting to her feet. "I'm gonna need a drink and a cigarette for this conversation." She was gone less than two minutes.

When she returned she had a lit cigarette in one hand and a glass of clear liquid in the other. Jared smelled the alcohol but said nothing.

"Did you have a good life? After I put you in the state home?"

"I was adopted by a couple from the country. They gave me the first home I'd ever known."

She thought about his words. "What's she like?" The words seemed hard for her to speak but after a slight pause she got them out. "Your mother."

"She bakes and sews and drives a tractor during harvest." Jared smiled thinking of her. "She grows vegetables and she took care of my dad when he had cancer. She dotes on her grandchildren."

Gloria nodded. "She sounds nice."

"She is."

"So…you married? Kids?"

"I was married recently and we're raising my sister's children." At the curious expression he added, "She was killed with her husband in a car accident."

She took another drink. "I'm sorry to hear that."

Jared was surprised because she actually sounded as though she meant it.

"Listen," she said a little too harshly, "I've waited a long time, wondering if I'd ever get the chance to tell you this so I'm just gonna go ahead and say it."

Jared was prepared for ugly recriminations about how she wished she had given him up sooner. He wasn't prepared for what he heard.

"I'm sorry." His expression must have registered surprise and shock. "About the last thing you expected to ever hear from me, isn't it?"

"Honestly? Yes."

She fell silent for a while and then sighed heavily swirling the liquid in the glass. "I should have had the guts to give you up when you were born," she said. "My mother warned me."

"I had a grandmother?"

"Don't get excited. She wasn't no more of a mother to me than I was to you…probably less of one." Another puff, another sip.

"But I was stubborn and determined. I'd be a better mother to you than she had been."

"You hated me…the things you said and did."

"I was neglectful," she admitted. "I was a loud-mouthed drunk who cared more about getting a date than getting a meal ready for her son. But I never hated *you*, Jared. I hated the fact that my mother was right. I'd turned out just like her."

"So you didn't keep me with you to punish me?"

She looked shocked. "Is that what you've thought all these years?" He nodded. "I kept you with me because while I could look at you I could convince myself I had done one good thing in my life. Why now? Why after so many years did you come looking for me?"

"I want to know if there was ever a time when you loved me."

He could see his question startled her. She cursed under her breath when she saw the glass was empty, but instead of going to refill it she put it on the table and crushed out her cigarette.

"I loved you when you were born," she said, matter-of-factly. "I looked down at you in my arms and I was going to give you the world."

"What happened?"

Her laugh was harsh. "Life happened. All those little things you don't think about when they hand you that baby in the delivery room, all snug and quiet and sweet. Money to buy food, diapers, rent for a roof over our heads. I can't even remember your father. Sometimes I'd meet a guy who didn't mind having a kid around, but they'd all get tired of a screaming baby eventually and I'd move on."

"I loved you most the day I let you go." Seeing he was the one surprised she added, "It's something you can't understand if you've never done it."

"You loved me but you still gave me up."

"And because I did you had a good life, a home, a family who cared about you. And look at you now. A man with a wife and children. Trust me, if you'd stayed with me, you'd have been in jail. You were already starting to mix with a bad crowd."

Jared could see for the first time that his mother wasn't a monster. She was a woman who'd made mistakes, a woman abandoned by everyone.

"Thank you."

She cast a curious glance at him. "What for?"

"For talking with me like this, for being honest. For giving me the chance all those years ago to have a normal life with a family who loves me."

She shrugged and gave him a nonchalant look. "Hey, I screwed up the rest of my life. I had to get something right eventually."

Jared hadn't planned to tell his mother so much about his life but the words tumbled out. "My wife…Annie, she had a baby when she was younger. She gave him up for adoption."

Gloria crossed her arms and leaned back in the chair. "And I can tell you have a problem with it."

"I've always had a problem with women giving their babies away."

"I guess I shoulder the blame for that. But if you want my advice, here it is—get over it."

Jared was stunned by her blunt, cold solution. "Just like that?"

She leaned forward, pinning him with a look. "What exactly is it you have the problem with? Are you upset that there was a man in her life before you? That she wasn't a virgin?"

"No." He spoke the truth. He'd been so caught up in

his reaction to finding out Annie's secret that he hadn't even given a thought to what he knew now had to have been that special relationship she'd briefly touched on.

"Did she have a good reason for giving him up?"

"She said she did."

"You didn't ask her?" When Jared didn't reply she sighed. "If you never believe another word I say, believe this. It is the hardest thing in the world to give up a child unless you're a woman devoid of any human feeling."

Just the kind of woman he'd always seen Gloria as.

"I can't imagine you falling in love and marrying someone like that," she said. "In fact, I'd say this girl must be something special."

"Why?"

"Because of the look on your face when you say her name, when you talk about her. Some of us go our whole lives and never see that look in a man's eyes."

Jared actually smiled. "I did something stupid."

Gloria laughed and for once it was a light sound. "You're human. You'd be genetically defective if you didn't do something stupid now and again. Is it fixable?"

"I think it might be…I hope it is."

She stood up and Jared did the same. "Then go home and fix whatever it is you did," she advised. "I spent my life running away from my problems, blaming everyone I could."

"Did you ever stop running?"

She nodded, looking at the ring on her left hand. "I found my anchor. It's the first commitment I've ever made in my life."

"You have to start somewhere."

"Yes, you do. Don't be too hard on your wife," she said. "It took courage to do what she did. Not all of us are that strong."

She closed the door and Jared stood there, smiling, for no other reason than it felt good to have the past where it belonged, in the background of his life.

He turned the car around at the end of the street and headed for home.

"He isn't back yet?"

Annie looked up when Caroline came into the den. She needed a break from staring at the computer screen. Sitting here had been a half-hearted attempt to do the budget for next month, but her thoughts had kept drifting.

"No, Possum, he's not."

"He didn't leave us."

It wasn't a question, it was a statement made with confidence. "Of course he didn't. He had things to do that couldn't wait."

"Annie?"

"Yes?"

"I heard you and Uncle Jared talking outside last night."

Annie held her arms out to the girl and she came into them. They hugged each other and eventually Caroline settled on Annie's knees.

"What did you hear?"

Annie stayed silent while Caroline recounted bits

and pieces of what had been said. She knew about Toby and she knew it had caused problems.

"I'm glad you gave us Toby," she said. "Mummy and Daddy got to do all the things with him that they missed out on with me and Luke. We weren't babies when we came here."

"Your mummy was my best friend when I was a little girl. I know you were worried a while back that you wouldn't remember her when you got older."

"Uncle Jared told you?"

"Yes. But you will, Caroline. You'll see a photograph and remember. You'll hear a song or see a flower and you'll remember."

"Grandma said sometimes when I'm not even trying to remember them, I will, anyway."

"She's right and memories are wonderful like that. We may not always use them, but when we need them to comfort us they'll always be there."

"I want Toby to know what she was like."

Annie did, too. She wanted the little boy upstairs to know how loved he was. "Then we'll make sure when he's older he knows. You can tell him all the things you remember and then they can be his memories, too."

"I love you, Annie."

Caroline hugged her so tightly Annie felt tears well in her eyes. "I love you, too, Caroline."

When the girl pulled back, she giggled. "I'm always making you cry."

"Tears of happiness, sweetie, that's all they are."

"That's the only kind we'll have around here from now on."

They both looked up at the familiar, deep voice.

"Uncle Jared!" Caroline ran to him, her arms going around him.

He hugged her tight. "Where are the boys?"

"Sleeping. Annie said I could stay up a little later tonight because there was a history program on."

He ruffled her hair. "How about you go get into bed?"

She looked warily from one to the other. "Remember what you said," she told him. "Only happy tears from now on."

The meaning of those words weren't lost on Jared as she left the room.

"I didn't hear you pull up." Annie pushed back the chair from the desk and walked toward him. "I was just working on the accounts."

Jared nodded but said nothing.

"She knows about Toby being my son," she said. "I'm sorry...I didn't mean for any of the children to find out."

Jared shoved his hands into the back pockets of his jeans and looked at her standing there. She was dressed for bed, the robe cinched around her petite frame, big fluffy white slippers on her feet and her hair pinned up.

"But it's the truth," he said finally. "You are Toby's mother. That isn't something that should be kept a secret."

Annie wondered where this was going. "Jared, if

you decide you can't continue to be married to me, I'll understand," she said, the words ripping from her. "But I'd like it if we could at least have Lewis draw up some arrangement that would allow me to still see the children."

He looked annoyed, and Annie wondered why. All she was trying to do was provide him with options.

"If I were divorcing you, Annie, we wouldn't need Lewis to draw up anything. Do you honestly think I'd stop you from being in the children's lives?"

"You were so angry when you found out about Toby," she explained. "Jared, was it just that I didn't tell you about Toby or that I'd gotten pregnant outside of marriage?"

"Believe it or not, when I stopped to think about it, I realized part of me was jealous that you had shared that part of yourself with another man."

"I was young," she said, trying to explain. "It's not an excuse…I had to come to terms with what I'd done and I feel that the Lord forgave me all my mistakes a long time before I was able to."

She came to stand in front of him. "Yes, I wanted to see Toby again, given the chance, but I didn't come here just to be with him again. I came here for all the children…for Sara and James. And I came here for you."

"Do you love me, Annie?"

"Yes."

"Are you in love with me?"

She wanted to look away, so tender were her feelings

for him. Instead she steeled herself and looked straight at him. "Yes, I am."

"That works out just fine," he replied. "Because you are the only woman I will ever love," he said, making sure he kept eye contact with her so there would be no doubt in her mind about his feelings.

Annie had been afraid to hope all day—she'd been going over various scenarios in her head but this hadn't been one of them.

"I'm sorry I didn't tell you at the start."

"If you had, I would have missed out on having you in my life because I would have ended it then and there and taken my chances with the social worker."

Guiding her to the small couch, Jared sat down with her tucked close beside him. He put his arm around her shoulder and took her hand and rested it palm-down on his thigh.

"Tell me about your life when you left here."

She looked up at him. "You really want to know? All of it?"

Jared didn't know if he was ready to hear more about Chris, especially now he knew they had been young lovers or if he could stand to hear how lonely she had been, or how tough her choices had been.

But whether he was ready to hear it or not, it was time that he did. "Start from the beginning and tell me what you feel comfortable with."

And she did. Annie was surprised. In the next two hours she told him about things in her life that were only brought to mind by the recounting of other times.

He alternately hugged her and kissed her head when she got to a tough recollection or a sad memory. And when she told him about the day Toby was born, he held her like he would never let her go.

Finally Annie wound down and couldn't remember ever having felt more mentally exhausted than she did now. Every part of her felt raw, laid bare.

But at least there were no more secrets.

"Thank you for sharing that with me." He pulled her more securely into the crook of his shoulder. "And I'm sorry I just took off like that last night."

Annie laid her head on his chest, listening to the steady strong beat of his heart. "It scared me, waking up to that note," she admitted.

"I went to see my mother."

Now it was her turn to hug him. She didn't look up, just tightened her arms around him. "Did it give you what you went looking for?"

He kissed the top of her head and inhaled the flowery scent of her shampoo. "Yes. I remembered her as this monster, uncaring and selfish."

"And?"

"Oh, she agreed with the selfish part, but only because she had kept me, thinking she could care for me. The reality is that she was alone, like you were, with a baby to raise that she was ill-equipped to deal with. She said the day she gave me up was when she loved me the most."

"I can understand that."

"I thought you would. She said you were a strong

woman, you had the courage to do what she didn't…and that was to do the best thing for your baby right from the start."

Now Annie did lift her head and look at him. "You told her about me?"

A wariness came into his eyes. "Was that wrong?"

She smiled. "No. Now you understand a little." She sat up then, pushing softly against his chest to look into those beautiful blue eyes that had captivated her from day one.

"Don't you see that Toby gave all of us something by being born? The lives he has touched are better because of it."

Annie was right…again. "I'm asking you to forgive me."

She frowned. "What on earth for?"

"I go to church, I try to live my life right and I know I screw things up," he said. "But I sat in judgment of you. Everyone could see it from a distant perspective but me. I want this marriage, Annie. I want our friendship and the relationship we were slowly building."

"So do I."

That made him smile. "And I'm willing to take is as slow as you want but…I love you Annie. I'm so in love with you I can't imagine a day without you."

"Oh, Jared, I'm in love with you, too. You're my best friend. You gave me a family, a home and a heart to belong to and grow old with. You've given me the world."

He looked down into her eyes and took the fall all over again. "Thank you for loving me, for helping me to face old fears. I could never have gone and seen my mother if the thought of losing you hadn't made me fight."

He hadn't been ready to give her up. "When Toby is old enough or when you feel ready, whichever comes first, I want him to know that you gave birth to him, that you're the reason he is here."

Annie felt the tears start to fall. "I don't ever want to take away from what Sara was."

"You won't. If I had to take a guess I'd say those kids will know more about Sara from the two of us than from anywhere else."

He sat forward and framed her face in his hands. "There is one question I have to ask you."

"Okay."

"Would you ever consider having another baby?"

Annie smiled. "Your baby?"

He shook his head. "*Our* baby."

"I would consider it very much," she said, throwing her arms around his neck. "You really want to have babies with me?"

"Well, not right away," he said, laughing as he held her. When she settled back down on the couch he kissed her forehead. "I'd like to wait until Toby is a little older."

"I think Caroline would like another girl around the house."

"Oh, I'm sure she would," he said, standing up and pulling her with him. "Let's go to bed."

They made it as far as the bottom of the stairs and then he stopped and kissed her, sweetly, gently…a prelude for all they would find with each other, all they would discover together.

"Don't ever stop loving me, Annie. I couldn't bear it."

"I could stop breathing easier than I could stop loving you," she replied. "In your heart, in your arms, I found my home and my family."

"In your eyes I see my future."

And as he climbed the stairs with Annie by his side, Jared viewed that future with a smile. It stretched out ahead of them, life in all its glory just waiting for them to experience it together.

God had given him Annie, and she had given him the love he had needed to face his fears and conquer the past. He knew how rare that kind of love was.

It was a gift he would never ever take for granted.

Epilogue

"Mummy! I wanna see the new baby!"

Jared scooped up his four-year-old daughter as she tried to jump on the hospital bed. "Not so fast, Miss Emily," he said, tickling her until she giggled.

She was a carbon copy of her father, all dark hair and mischievous eyes. Caroline followed Jared into the room, Jamie in her arms. He was Emily's twin but the only thing they shared was a birthday. He was a quiet child, his red hair and freckles making him stand out from the crowd.

Luke stood at the end of the bed while Toby came up and stood near his mother. "Daddy said it came last night," he said, awestruck as he had been with his other two younger siblings.

"Yes, *she* did."

He looked sad. "I wanted a brother."

"Tough luck, squirt," said Caroline, taking Jamie back into her arms. "We needed another girl to even up the numbers."

"Are you feeling okay?"

Annie nodded and smiled at Luke's inquiry. At twelve, he was as tall as his uncle. He also was now more quietly spoken and had a lot of Jared's mannerisms learned over the years.

Annie looked at her family. "I'm feeling fine," she said. Sometimes it was hard to believe how Caroline and Luke had grown.

Caroline, now almost fourteen, was a straight-A student more interested in archaeology than in the latest music and fashion, though she did try to keep up. Luke was a born farmer like his uncle, his love for the land evident in every hour he spent by Jared's side.

"Of course, I'd feel even finer if my husband would get over here and give me a kiss."

The kids giggled, Caroline rolled her eyes and Luke blushed. But Jared kissed her, anyway. One hour ago she'd been telling him she couldn't possibly push just one more time.

Like the two children before her, Amy Catherine Campbell had taken her sweet time about coming into the world, and each time Annie had been the bravest woman he knew

In five years she had given him the kind of life he could only have dreamed of before. She'd given him love, a safe haven to come to at the end of each day and loving arms to hold him.

And this morning she had given him another precious child, another daughter to worry about and marvel over.

"Hi there, Gorgeous."

"She's not gorgeous, she's Mummy," said Emily.

Jared smiled. "She'll always be gorgeous to me."

Annie didn't feel gorgeous. She felt like she'd been run down by a truck. But she also knew in the nursery down the hall lay a precious little bundle of life.

It was all worth it—the pain, the exhaustion, the pushing. And Jared had been there with her this time as he had been every time before.

"Where's the baby, Mummy?"

"She's right here," said the nurse, bringing the newest member of the family in and placing her in her mother's arms. "She had her first bath and did fine."

The nurse disappeared as the kids milled around, the smaller ones making sounds of awe, Luke getting that protective look that he had for Emily and Caroline, a mirror image of the one his uncle wore many times.

Caroline smiled. "You have beautiful babies."

"I have beautiful children," she corrected, reaching out and taking hold of Caroline's hand briefly. "All my children."

Jared set Emily on the edge of the bed and took his daughter from Annie, holding her so gently. Annie loved the contrast, she always did. The large, strong man and the tiny bundle that fit in his hands so perfectly. It was while Emily was saying hello to her new little sister that the proud grandparents arrived, Lewis trailing behind them.

Eve's eyes misted when she saw the newest addition. "She's beautiful. You do very good work."

Annie chuckled. "I had a little help."

Lewis rolled his eyes with a wry smile. "Now I have to change the will again!"

"You're leaving me the car, though," said Luke.

Caroline laughed. "And you promised me the apartment."

Lewis held up his hands feigning a defensive gesture. "Hey, can we all just wait until I depart this earth before we start divvying up my assets?"

It was an old joke, one she'd heard many times before.

Annie lay back, content to watch her family welcome the newest member. This was what life was all about. Life for her was family, faith and commitment.

It was about building a solid foundation.

Life with Jared had turned out to be God's greatest gift to her, among the many He had bestowed upon her. He had stood beside her when they had told Toby about his birth. He'd been with her for the birth of their children. It seemed every time she looked for him she didn't have to look far, he was always there, smiling, encouraging and loving her.

He'd taken to the role of fatherhood naturally after learning the first steps with Caroline, Luke and Toby. But the wonder in his face when he'd seen his children born was something that would stay with her forever.

Right now he was making his way toward her bed, having handed Emily to her doting grandmother. While everyone circled around Eve, Jared just looked at her.

"I'm proud of what you did in there, Annie. Just

when I think you can't amaze me, all over again you prove me wrong."

Annie took his hand in hers. "You helped. You don't know how much it means to me when I'm going through that to look up and see you there telling me I can go just a little extra."

He leaned down and kissed her softly on the lips. "Happy anniversary and thank you for my gift."

"Happy anniversary," she replied. Their celebration dinner last night had been interrupted by her water breaking. "And you're welcome."

"I love you, Annie, with all my heart."

She felt it in every word he spoke to her, in every touch he gave her, and she saw it every time he looked at her.

"I love you, too."

"Forever," he reminded her.

"At least that long."

He kissed her one more time, perching himself on the edge of the bed, his arm around her. He sat there watching his family, watching the love and knowing that he had God to thank for bringing Annie into his life five years ago.

Without her none of this would have been possible.

She was the fire that lit the flame that warmed them all. That flame was called family and it burned ever brighter in their house, fuelled by hard work, commitment and love.

Their blessings were many, their love a lasting one.

* * * * *

And now, turn the page for
a sneak preview of

WINDIGO TWILIGHT,

the first book in the
GREAT LAKES LEGENDS *miniseries*
by Colleen Rhoads,

part of Steeple Hill's exciting new line,
Love Inspired Suspense!
On sale in August 2005 from Steeple Hill Books.

Prologue

The sun threw a last golden glow across the horizon of Lake Superior. From her vantage point about five miles from Eagle Island, Suzanne Baxter could see nothing but the cold, clear waters of the big lake they call Gitchee Gummee.

She leaned against the railing of the forty-foot yacht and lifted her face to the breeze. Her husband, Mason, joined her.

"I'm glad we came," she said, turning to slip her arms around his still-trim body. Even at fifty-four, he could still make her heart race like a teenager's. They'd come through so much over the years.

He dropped a kiss on top of her head. "Me, too. It was time to make amends."

She bristled. "You mean let them make amends. You didn't do anything."

"Don't start," he said. "It was the right thing to do."

"I'm not so sure anyone but your mother feels that

way. The rest stand to lose a lot of money with you back in your mother's good graces. She intends to leave you the lion's share now as her only living child." She pulled away and rubbed her arms.

"They'll get used to it." He swept his hand over the railing. "I can't believe we allowed ourselves to be gone from this for fifteen years. The kids should have been here every summer."

"We'll all come out in August. Jake will be done with his dig by mid-July, and Wynne's dive should be over about the same time. Becca will be out of school. I miss them."

"We'll be home by Wednesday. You could call Becca on the ship-to-shore phone. She should be around."

Suzanne hesitated. She'd like nothing better than to share things with her youngest child, but something still didn't feel right about the situation. She'd caught undercurrents at the old manor house, eddies of danger she wasn't about to share with her daughter yet. Becca would just worry. "I'll see her in a few days," she said.

He nodded and pulled her back against his chest as they watched the sun plunging into the water.

A rumble started under her feet, a vibration that made her toes feel tingly. It radiated up her calves. "What is that?" she asked Mason.

He frowned. His hand began to slide from her waist as he turned to check it out. But the rumble became a roar as the hull of the boat burst apart. The explosion tossed Suzanne into the air. As she hurtled toward the frigid Lake Superior water, her last regretful thought was of her children.

Chapter One

"I applied for a job on the island." Waiting for a response from her siblings on the three-way conference call, Rebecca Baxter gripped her cordless phone until her fingers cramped. No telling how loud the opposition would be, though it was in her favor that her brother was in Montserrat and her sister in Argentina.

The answering hum on the line made her wonder if the conference call with her siblings had gotten disconnected. Then she heard Jake's long sigh and braced herself for his reaction.

"You're not going anywhere. The estate isn't settled yet, and you promised to do it," Jake said.

Her brother's reaction was surprisingly mild, but after twenty-five years, Becca knew he was the maddest when he was the quietest.

"I had a phone interview this afternoon, and it went great. Not many people know about the Ojibwa culture and not many would be willing to go to a deserted island in the middle of Lake Superior. I'm pretty sure I'll get the job." Her voice didn't even tremble, and she gave herself a thumbs-up approval. She couldn't let them know how terrified she really was. This was the new Becca—strong and courageous.

"Jake, settle down." Her sister Wynne's soft voice was mellow enough to tame him. As head of an archeological team, Jake sometimes forgot his sisters didn't have to jump at his command, not even Becca, the youngest.

"Don't encourage her!" This time there was no doubt about his displeasure.

Becca winced and held the phone out from her ear for a moment then put it back. "You can't stop me, Jake. Max Duncan seemed very impressed with my credentials." Even if he sounded as gruff as a grizzly bear. She grimaced and waited for the next objection.

"That was cousin Laura's husband, right?" Wynne asked. "He's still there even though she's dead?"

"Yep. He's a writer. I found out he was researching a new novel set on an Ojibwa reservation and offered my expertise."

Jake snorted. "A perfect job for a career student like you. You've done some harebrained things in the past, but we're both too far away to bail you out of trouble this time."

"Jake," Wynne warned again.

"Okay, she just caught me off-guard." His voice softened. "You seem so certain the explosion wasn't an accident. I'm not so sure, Becca. You don't have a shred of evidence."

Defensive hackles raised along Becca's back. Jake was a man of science who would scoff at the way she felt things. "I know it in my heart," she said quietly. "I'm not going to let them get away with it."

"I think it's just the way you're dealing with Mom and Dad's deaths. No one rigged the boat to blow. It was an accident."

Becca thought her brother's emphatic announcement was his way of convincing himself, but she kept that opinion to herself.

"Gram will recognize you," Wynne said.

It was Becca's main fear. "I applied as Becca Lynn and left off my last name altogether. I was ten the last time I saw her, and everyone was still calling me Becky. Besides, Max mentioned she was away on a trip to Europe. I've got four weeks to find out who killed them."

"Max and Laura had a little girl, didn't they?" Wynne's voice was thoughtful.

"Molly. She's five. She would have been only two when Laura died."

"There was some question that maybe Max had killed her, wasn't there? I don't like this, Becca." Wynne sounded worried.

Becca could picture her older sister clearly. She missed Wynne with a sudden pang. The funeral a month ago had been a kaleidoscope of pain and disbelief where mourners and family moved though the landscape in a blur of pats and hugs. There had been no real time to grieve together.

No one from the island had come. The thought made

her press her lips together and scowl. Gram had outlived all three sons. The least Gram could have done was bid her last son farewell.

The lump in her throat grew until she wasn't sure she could speak. Becca sipped her licorice tea, cold now with a gray scum on top. The call waiting beeped, and she glanced at it. "I have to go. Max is calling me back. I'll let you know when I get to Windigo Manor."

She clicked the button and answered the new call. "Becca Lynn."

"When can you come?" Max Duncan's deep voice asked.

"Immediately," she answered. As she made arrangements to be picked up at the boat dock, she wondered what she was getting herself into. But she had to try.

Dear Reader,

Though I didn't know it at the time, the seed for this story was planted over twenty years ago, long before I ever thought of becoming a writer. I grew up in a large and loving family, the baby of six. My parents were a gift in my life, loving, caring and wise.

But there was a young woman whose love had already changed my life and would do so in the future, in ways I could not yet imagine. I've learned a lot about her in the years since. I know she carried me in her thoughts and her heart until her last day on this earth. I know that I look like her and that we would have been great friends.

Her gift to me were many—the gift of life; parents who kept me safe and loved me; brothers and sisters who gave me nieces and nephews to spoil and adore. But there was more awaiting me—a baby sister, aunts, an uncle, cousins and grandparents.

Today I live halfway around the world, and am married to a wonderful man whose family has surrounded me with their love. I burn up the telephone wires between the U.S. and Australia on a regular basis but time and distance have only made my family ties stronger.

The dynamics of what makes up a family may be ever-changing in society but the threads that keep them strong will always remain—faith, acceptance, commitment and love. I hope you enjoy this journey with Jared and Annie.

Best wishes

Mary Kate Holder

Take 2 inspirational love stories FREE!

PLUS get a FREE surprise gift!

Mail to Steeple Hill Reader Service™

In U.S.	In Canada
3010 Walden Ave.	P.O. Box 609
P.O. Box 1867	Fort Erie, Ontario
Buffalo, NY 14240-1867	L2A 5X3

YES! Please send me 2 free Love Inspired® novels and my free surprise gift. After receiving them, if I don't wish to receive anymore, I can return the shipping statement marked cancel. If I don't cancel, I will receive 4 brand-new novels every month, before they're available in stores! Bill me at the low price of $4.24 each in the U.S. and $4.74 each in Canada, plus 25¢ shipping and handling and applicable sales tax, if any*. That's the complete price and a savings of over 10% off the cover prices—quite a bargain! I understand that accepting the books and gift places me under no obligation ever to buy any books. I can always return a shipment and cancel at any time. Even if I never buy another book from Steeple Hill, the 2 free books and the surprise gift are mine to keep forever.

113 IDN DZ9M
313 IDN DZ9N

Name	(PLEASE PRINT)	
Address	Apt. No.	
City	State/Prov.	Zip/Postal Code

Not valid to current Love Inspired® subscribers.

Want to try two free books from another series?
Call 1-800-873-8635 or visit www.morefreebooks.com.

* Terms and prices are subject to change without notice. Sales tax applicable in New York. Canadian residents will be charged applicable provincial taxes and GST. All orders subject to approval. Offer limited to one per household.

® are registered trademarks owned and used by the trademark owner and or its licensee.

INTLI04R   ©2004 Steeple Hill

Love Inspired®

HIS UPTOWN GIRL

BY

GAIL SATTLER

She didn't look like a mechanic…yet model-perfect Georgette Ecklington was the best in town. Her boss, Bob Delanio, was attracted to his newest employee, but he knew he didn't belong in her privileged world. It wouldn't be an easy task for Georgette to convince her handsome downtown boss to take a risk on an uptown girl!

Don't miss HIS UPTOWN GIRL
On sale July 2005

Available at your favorite retail outlet.